QUAKER
SILENCE

QUAKER SILENCE

By

IRENE ALLEN

VILLARD BOOKS, NEW YORK 1992

Library of Congress Cataloging-in-Publication Data
Allen, Irene
Quaker silence / by Irene Allen.—1st ed.
p.   cm.
ISBN 0-679-41414-2
I. Title.
PS3551.L3935Q3 1992
813'.54—dc20   92-1359

9 8 7 6 5 4 3 2
First Edition
Book design by Elizabeth Fox

FOR SARAH AND CLIFFORD

Acknowledgments

The idea for this book germinated as I lay in a hospital bed at Harvard University. I had sought medical care for a few days, but days turned into weeks and weeks turned into months. My daydreams about writing would not have survived the regimentation of the hospital were it not for enlivening visitations from Members and Attenders of Friends Meeting at Cambridge. It is a pleasure to acknowledge the help and hope given to me by Friends in the darkness of that summer. May the character of Elizabeth Elliot capture a part of my visitors' concern and patience! My thanks to: Patricia Watson; Seamus Kearney; Marilyn Neyer, John and Joel; Christopher Curtis; Elizabeth Coxe; and Clifford Harrison.

My parents helped me to make the transition from lying in a bed to sitting at a desk and writing. Using mysterious processes known only to Baptists, they have restored my health. Any thanks I can give are inadequate.

Several Friends in New England and Pennsylvania read the manuscript of this book and improved my explanations of Quaker thought and practices. I am responsible for the errors that remain.

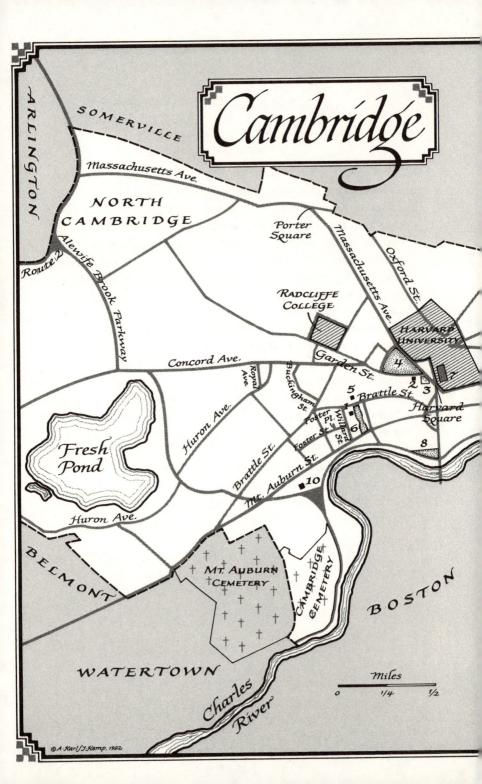

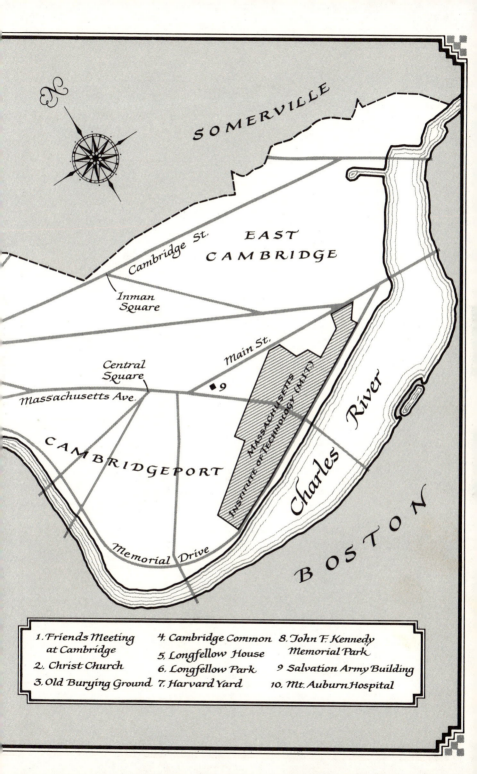

SOMERVILLE

EAST CAMBRIDGE

Cambridge St.

Inman Square

Central Square

Main St.

■ 9

Massachusetts Ave.

MASSACHUSETTS INSTITUTE OF TECHNOLOGY (M.I.T.)

C A M B R I D G E P O R T

Charles River

Memorial Drive

B O S T O N

1. Friends Meeting at Cambridge
2. Christ Church
3. Old Burying Ground
4. Cambridge Common
5. Longfellow House
6. Longfellow Park
7. Harvard Yard
8. John F. Kennedy Memorial Park
9. Salvation Army Building
10. Mt. Auburn Hospital

QUAKER SILENCE

I

The intent of all speaking is to bring into the life, and to walk in, and to possess the same, and to live in and enjoy it, and to feel God's presence.

George Fox, Founder of Quakerism, 1657

Elizabeth Elliot shifted her sixty-six-year-old bones slightly forward on the hard bench to ease her arthritic back pain brought on by the October frost. But she felt, on the whole, remarkably well. Sunday mornings often brought peace to Elizabeth, and this morning she felt a strong sense of being at home. A physically strong woman with two grown sons, she had the comfort of having met well the challenges of life. Her sons had grown up differently from what she had expected, but they were responsible and able men. The younger, Andrew, worked as an engineer in Cambridge. The elder, Mark, was a pediatric resident in Boston. He and his wife had recently had a baby, Elizabeth's first grandchild. Elizabeth had had her losses and pains, of course: she had been a widow for six years now. But she had adapted to widowhood, helped by her religious faith.

Elizabeth looked around the silent Quaker Meeting in which she sat, enjoying the Sunday morning sun slanting through the windows of an old New England Meetinghouse. She had walked to Meeting in bright sunlight. A few birds had been chirping, and because it was Sunday automobile traffic was not heavy. The sun and the quiet of her walk were still with Elizabeth as she looked around. About one hundred Quakers were gathered together. The worship had been entirely silent, which was not uncommon in Friends Meeting at Cambridge. A lifelong Quaker, Elizabeth had the responsibility today to decide when the silence had reached its natural end. Occasionally this was not an easy judgment and, mindful of that, she returned to prayer.

The silence of Quaker prayer had always been a two-edged sword in Elizabeth's life. Deep silence sometimes gave her comfort, but this solace was not without costs. If her conscience was troubling her, Elizabeth actually had a dread of Meeting, for in worshipful silence she had heard the harshest criticism she knew in life. But never had Quaker prayer led her into feelings of despair. She found in the silence the ever-present possibility of absolution and renewal. Although the struggle toward grace could be long and painful, Elizabeth did not doubt it could be successful and the journey of life could be completed in God's care.

Across the room, a scrawny, eight-year-old boy named Jack Nelson looked out the window. He always liked to sit next to a window so that when things got tedious, he at least had recourse to some visual freedom. His mother allowed him to choose their seats. She did her best to keep him still, so as not to disturb the worship. Jack swung his feet back and forth under the bench. He began to drum his fingers on the seat in front of him, an activity his mother immediately stopped. Jack's mother, Alice, remembered a time when she had been young and childless. In those days, she used to think that Quakers should be celibate or adopt children over eighteen years old. Only then would Sunday morning's Meeting for Worship be truly silent. But, as it happened, she had her own child now and had the task of bringing him up within Quaker practice as best she could. It was difficult to control an eight-year-old boy for an hour without speaking to him. If things had been more satisfactory with Jack's development, he would have been in First-day school. But Jack did not like elementary school, and indeed had been held back the previous year. No sort of Sunday school had worked well for him; he needed individual attention and encouragement. His mother, in an attempt to maintain some sort of spiritual life for herself, now brought Jack to Meeting for Worship despite the difficulties in keeping him quiet.

Jack's attention shifted outside the window: a blue jay had just landed on the grass near the sidewalk of Longfellow Park. The jay pecked furiously at something on the ground which Jack could not clearly see. Fully absorbed, the boy sat still; his mother, glancing at him, momentarily relaxed a bit.

Alice looked across the Meetinghouse at the new Clerk, Elizabeth Elliot. To Alice's critical eye, Elizabeth was a bit overweight and certainly not tall. But she had an open and pleasant face, somehow always near to smiling, a comforting face topped with a thick thatch of gray hair. Alice mused that Elizabeth looked as friendly and warm as she, in fact, was. Elizabeth was still vigorous enough to accept the demanding job as Clerk of the Meeting. Alice hoped she would have as much energy when she reached her sixties. Sometimes she felt that raising Jack must be taking a decade off her life. Looking back at her son, Alice put her hand on his knee as a warning not to swing his legs under the bench. Her thoughts in the silence centered on the effort to raise her son in these violent and difficult times. She had the added burden of raising him as a single mother and felt the need of her community's help and support in that undertaking. She was grateful for Meeting and hoped her son would find, in time, something for himself in Quaker silence.

Sitting in front of Jack and his mother, a young, homeless man named Tim rocked slowly back and forth. The rocking did not reflect boredom, but a restlessness Tim could not have explained. Tim spent his day wandering among half a dozen soup kitchens and places he panhandled, never having more than distant friendships and never finding a place where he could feel at home. Throughout most of the year, he slept on the grass of Longfellow Park near the Meetinghouse. Soup kitchens around Harvard Square gave him meals. Tim was a big man: six foot one and broad shouldered, he looked strong. However, as his time on the streets increased, he was losing some vigor. His face was beginning to hint at a gauntness that would surely grow. For him, October meant the return of cold nights spent sleeping on the heating grates of Harvard University's larger buildings. But, by Tim's standards, things would not get really bad until November's sleet and snow arrived.

Tim, whose last name was unknown in the Meeting, was a bright and sometimes articulate man. He often spoke at Meeting for Worship, standing and holding forth on a number of topics centered on poverty. His speech in Meeting was often antagonistic and distressed some Friends. Worse still, he was sometimes almost violent in tone. This was a great challenge for pacifist Quakers to accept. Despite several years' effort, the Meeting community had not found a comfortable way to respond to him. Tim felt rejected by individual Quakers, but he continued to come to Meeting because it was a place of relative calm. He could not express what it was he found in Quaker stillness, but he willingly returned each Sunday.

In the early days of his coming to Meeting, Tim's speech was somewhat detached from reality. Certainly he lived with voices other than those most people heard. Lately, however, Tim had fewer detached spells. This morning Tim sighed as he rocked and felt only mildly uneasy about his nearest neighbors on the bench. He knew that some wondered if he came on Sundays because of the lunch served after Meeting. But he could have had a better meal later in the afternoon from the Catholic church only a few blocks away, and it hurt Tim that the people he sat next to did not respect his motives for coming to Meeting. As he sat in the stillness, Tim decided he had some good reasons to feel depressed. The Quakers around him sensed both his unhappiness and their partial responsibility for it. The silence continued.

At the head of the room, Elizabeth thought about Tim with real concern. She wondered how he was managing at night now that the frost was returning. She also hoped that he would not cause a disturbance as the worship period neared its end. In the past, Tim's speeches, especially his most distressing ones, had come right at the end of the worship hour. Elizabeth had known Tim for several years, as long as he had been coming to Meeting. She liked him for his independence, and for his obvious ability to survive the pain that life brought. Elizabeth had spoken to Tim off and on for several years and sensed that much of his distress stemmed from severe family troubles. During the time she had known him, Tim had progressed considerably toward a more normal existence.

Elizabeth respected Tim. She believed he was engaged in a serious spiritual quest. His frequent attendance at Meeting for Worship over several years indicated to her that he sought the Spirit. No greater accomplishment, in Elizabeth's eyes, was possible for anyone. She knew little about theories of mental illness. She wished she and other Quakers could better ease the torment which gripped Tim, but she did not dismiss him as "ill" in the same way many members of the Meeting did. Elizabeth thought that all people had some degree of psychological troubles. God, in her view, did not fail to communicate to men like Tim merely because they were more distressed than some of their neighbors. She found Tim a source of inspiration for the Meeting as well as a source of problems; she worked hard at listening to what he said in Meeting and had some success in speaking to him afterward.

About the time that Tim began to rock back and forth, a young woman near the center of the room also began to grow restless. Sarah Curtis, Elizabeth Elliot's niece, was a good-looking woman with braided blond hair. A trim and physically active student, she looked like a picture in a health club ad. She had been raised a Quaker, attending Friends schools in New York City from kindergarten onwards. She was now a junior at Harvard, majoring in natural science and probably headed for medical school. But she had begun reading women's literature and taking classes in women's studies the previous semester, finding such things more relevant and more interesting than organic chemistry. She was restless this morning because she had brought her friend Steve to Meeting. They had known each other since her freshman year and had started going out together last spring. Things were now getting serious between them.

Steve was a senior at Harvard. He was Jewish and went to the Friday evening Hillel. In fact, he was one of the readers for the services. Sarah was nervous about how he was reacting to the Meeting. Normally several Friends spoke. This morning's complete silence, Sarah feared, might be disorienting to a visitor. She wondered if she should take his hand, but decided some Quakers would be offended by such an action. Sarah shifted her weight and looked at Elizabeth, wondering if she would soon close the Meeting.

Just then, an older man on a back bench rose and looked around. Tall and lean, he had a full head of gray hair, cut short and neatly combed. His suit was a conservative gray, much darker than his hair. Only his tie showed a little subdued color. John Hoffman had been a member of

Cambridge Meeting since the 1940s. He spoke in Meeting only rarely, but on this day, clearing his throat and taking a deep breath, he began.

"Friends, I feel I must speak this morning. Anyone as old as I am tends to look back at life. I've been revising my will this weekend and making arrangements to retire, and I've had a lot to consider about how I have spent my days.

"My business life has always been full and profitable. I've always told myself that I was working for the enjoyment of the work and the challenge of business decisions. But now that I look at all my assets and holdings, I think it only fair to say I have spent much of my life making money for the sake of making money."

Here John Hoffman paused. The strain of saying what he felt showed in his face. His sharp features displayed deep concentration. Taking a slow breath, he continued.

"As a good Quaker, I have always lived quite simply. No one can say I flaunted my wealth or have been a spendthrift in any way, and I've always given to good causes, including this Meeting. But it is still true that I willingly made a lot of money, and I have let it pile up as life went along.

"I don't think I'm alone in this. We Quakers are a wealthy denomination; I think only the Episcopalians can rival us. Why does the Quaker tradition permit this so easily when in other areas we are much more thoughtful? We are cautious and concerned in all questions regarding violence and war, but we don't have a strong tradition of examining the consequences of our economic lives.

"What I wonder now is why I have spent my life pursuing something none of us would defend." John paused again. He looked around, almost sadly, and continued. "My old will and financial plans, which I was rereading last week, certainly don't address my present concerns about the corruption and personal limitations that wealth brings. I guess I'm trying to say I need to reexamine all questions related to money and decide what to do at this point. I hope Friends will consider what they're doing with their financial lives and ask themselves how they can respond to the gospel in a more thoughtful way than I have done."

After speaking, John Hoffman sat down rather stiffly. There was a sober and thick stillness in the room. William Hoffman, nephew of the speaker, wondered what his uncle had in mind. Today's vocal ministry was quite foreign to Bill. He was a lawyer in Cambridge, was well off, and felt no qualms about it. He had just been nominated to be a judge for the Commonwealth of Massachusetts, the culmination of many years of careful legal work and political maneuvering with the governor's office. Quakers did not understand Bill's professional life; it had many elements with which the Society of Friends was often not identified. But they knew Bill as a serious and responsible man who worked hard for the Meeting in several ways. Although he had no wife and children, he valued family life. He was known to keep in touch with at least one distant Quaker relative, and he often spent time with his uncle.

Bill handled the legal work his uncle's business generated. He therefore knew his uncle had previously intended to leave a good part of his money to the Meeting and to Swarthmore College, his alma mater. The remainder of his estate was to go to Bill himself, as John's nearest relative. This seemed to be an orderly and reasonable arrangement to the lawyer, and he was sure it would seem so to other Quakers. Bill hoped his uncle's newfound doubts were not as deep as his speech today might indicate, and he thought perhaps these doubts would pass quickly. Bill determined to speak to his uncle after worship.

Elizabeth was startled but impressed by what John Hoffman had said. It seemed the Spirit had truly been behind his speaking. Thankful for the message, she tried to hold it in her heart. The silence prodded more seriously at Elizabeth's mind, and she examined herself again in light of what John had said. Considerations about money always pulled her in two directions. She sturdily resisted going further into what the silence seemed to be pointing toward this morning.

Several minutes ticked by on the Clerk's watch, but no one else felt called to speak. The Clerk closed the Meeting by shaking hands with her neighbor, the customary signal for all present to shake hands with those sitting nearby. Elizabeth rose to welcome any newcomers and made several announcements about events of the coming week. As usual, at the close of the announcements, the Meetinghouse erupted into sound as people stood up, chatting with neighbors, slowly making their way out. The contrast to the silence was sharp, and Elizabeth wondered, for the thousandth time, what such an abrupt change from deep silence to clamoring sounds might mean about what modern Quakers really valued.

Young Jack, who had been sitting on the edge of his bench when Elizabeth had made the announcements, slipped quickly through the adults as the noise began. He ran out into the Meetinghouse yard to enjoy the fall day. Tim also made his way to the door. No eyes met his as he moved through the room and no hands extended toward him in greeting. Sucking in his breath, he shook his head. He felt more alone than he had for a long time. Like Jack, Tim went out into the yard to see what could be made of the sunlight and to wait for the sandwiches and coffee that would soon be served from the kitchen in an adjacent building.

Sarah, taking Steven by the hand, went out the side door of the Meetinghouse, away from the crowds gathered in the yard and spilling into Longfellow Park. They went over to a bench beside the tiny parking lot behind the Meetinghouse and sat down.

"Was it OK?" asked Sarah.

"Yes," said Steven, "at least it wasn't offensive. In fact, I don't think it even seemed Christian. Nobody mentioned Jesus!"

"Sometimes people quote from the New Testament, sometimes from the Old. Sometimes there's just silent prayer. But most Quakers think in New Testament terms."

"Tell me again, what's the silence for?" asked Steven.

"It's one of the easiest ways to hear God's voice," said Sarah. "But I think it takes some getting used to. If you want," she continued, "we can get a copy of the book which gives the official Quaker line about the silence."

"I can't read Quaker propaganda. Don't ask me to do that! Anyway, being silent for an hour is pretty weird, if you ask me."

"The basic idea comes from Jewish Scripture, you know. Quakers think of what they do as 'waiting on the Lord.' Remember all those Old Testament verses like 'They who wait upon the Lord will be renewed in strength'? That one is from Isaiah, but there are lots more."

"My memory of that stuff is a little vague. Isaiah was only a prophet, you know. It's not part of the first five books. But if the silence is waiting, is someone supposed to show up to end the waiting? Like the Messiah?"

"The theory is that Jesus was the Messiah"—Sarah laughed—"and He's already come. That's the part you can't accept, and I don't blame you, but that's what Friends think. Jesus comes to Meeting, by the way. He's there in spirit. Otherwise it wouldn't be a Meeting with a capital *M*."

"So then there's no need to wait for him?" asked Steven with exasperation.

"It's like Zen, stupid. You wait until the waiting itself is worthwhile. There's some deep things in that silence. Anyway, it's the Lord you're waiting on, not Jesus."

"I'll never understand the trinity," he said with disgust. "Monotheism is so much simpler!"

"Steven, what are you and me going to do in the long run?" asked Sarah as she rose to her feet. "Having this between us is a pain in the butt!"

"The only solution," he replied, also standing up, "is for you to convert. Become one of the chosen people!"

"I already am chosen, thank you," said Sarah vehemently. Steven was standing up to join her. "Come on," she said in a different tone, "let's go to Harvard Square and get something to eat. I've got a lot of chem homework this afternoon and I haven't touched it for a week."

"I thought the person making the announcements said we could eat here," said Steven.

"She's my aunt Elizabeth, by the way. Uncle Michael died some years back, when I was a kid," she added. "But yes, we can eat here, if you don't mind peanut butter and jelly and some kind of veggie soup."

"Sounds fine to me, and it'll be a lot faster than Harvard Square on a Sunday." Hand in hand the pair walked off in the direction of the kitchen. Sarah's mind turned for the moment from the Steven problem to general dread of the chemistry assignments which awaited her back in her room on campus.

The person most impressed by what John Hoffman had said stood near the Meetinghouse door waiting for him to emerge. Adam Chrisler, with an emotional and vocal temperament, was an iconoclastic sort of Quaker. As a youth, he had protested the Vietnam War, spending several months in jail for it. He still participated in protests at a consulting firm which tested nerve gas equipment in Cambridge, and he refused to pay the portion of federal income tax which went for military purposes. On most matters up for discussion in the Meeting, he and John Hoffman were on opposite sides. Indeed, if Adam and John agreed on something, it was felt by the members that either a mistake must have occurred or God's will must truly and directly have been revealed.

Adam waited by the door until John came through and then held out his hand, saying, "Good morning! Thanks for your message in worship! I'm glad you felt moved to speak." Adam knew that many Friends thought it inappropriate to thank an individual for a message which had, after all, been given by the Spirit. But there were many Quaker rules which Adam was used to bending.

John felt awkward about what had been said but replied, "I'm certainly looking at things differently these days."

Not wishing to appear as if he were too pleased, Adam smiled again but turned away from John to speak to Elizabeth Elliot, who had just emerged from the main door. Tim, who was still in the middle of the yard and had seen Adam's brief conversation with John, now watched John walk toward Longfellow Park. Tim felt anger against Hoffman because of what he had said in Meeting.

Elizabeth Elliot greeted Adam and asked if she could get herself a cup of tea, promising to return and speak to him in a moment. In the kitchen of the adjacent building she procured a cup of Lipton's and took a dose of blood pressure medicine with her first sip. She felt the need of a dose of her arthritis medicine as well, but could not take it on an empty stomach. She returned outside to Adam and the two walked a few yards away from the Meetinghouse so that they could speak more privately. Elizabeth always liked to talk to Adam alone. Adam, a free-lance writer, sometimes wrote for rather dubious periodicals. Elizabeth found his opinions, and to some extent his behavior, unpredictable. She, who had been a Quaker long before the 1960's anti-war movement brought peace issues into the mainstream of American politics, felt some distrust of Adam and other Friends who had converted in the sixties. She often lectured herself to trust people like Adam more, but her lectures had still not overcome all her prejudices.

Elizabeth thought she knew what was on Adam's mind, and she rather dreaded this conversation. Adam had strong opinions about what the Meeting should be doing regarding political and social questions. He was not as well known, however, for coming to Meetings for Worship or Meetings for Healing. But she knew it was best to try to understand what he cared deeply about.

This afternoon, after the simple lunch, there would be a Meeting for Business. Sometimes these Meetings were quite routine, as when the building committee asked for a small amount of money to repair some cracked window-panes. Sometimes the Business Meetings were long and emotional, as when Friends tried to decide whether they would marry people of the same sex.

The issue of same-sex marriage had been before Cambridge Quakers for two years now. Elizabeth Elliot, as Clerk, chaired the Business Meetings. This unenviable task made it her responsibility to guide Quakers toward what Friends called a "sense of the Meeting." Quakers prided themselves on making decisions, great and small, on this basis: following the Spirit found in all persons. While it was possible to reach this goal in some matters, a truly Spirit-led decision could be difficult even for dedicated Quakers in questions or problems charged with emotion. Such issues included illegal actions and protests and questions of sexuality.

As Elizabeth had suspected, Adam Chrisler had the Business Meeting on his mind.

"Several committee reports are listed on the agenda before the same-sex marriage question, Friend. This has happened in the past with bad results. We just won't have enough time for it unless it goes first in the order of business," Adam said.

"It's not appropriate to change the agenda at this late hour," replied Elizabeth. "The committee reports listed are each important to different members, and we need to hear them this afternoon." The Clerk smiled hopefully at Adam and continued, "But none of the committee reports is long, at least so I have been assured, and I'm confident that the Meeting will have plenty of time to discuss the marriage question at length."

Adam looked unconvinced, but he heard finality in her voice. He accepted what the Clerk had said as gracefully as he could and excused himself to go hunt up a cup of the Meeting's coffee.

About the same time, Jack, having chased away all the blue jays in Longfellow Park, was wandering back toward the Meetinghouse looking for his mother. He wondered if they could go home now or if she would stay for lunch and Business Meeting. He decided to ask his mother if he could walk home if she insisted on staying. He paused at the edge of the park because two Quaker men were arguing loudly with each other. Jack did not pay much attention to the adults in Meeting, and he did not recognize the two. But he did recognize that such a heated argument was an unusual event, and he was sufficiently frightened by the ugliness in the men's voices to hurry toward the Meetinghouse without looking back. As he rounded the bushes in front of the building he almost collided with Sarah and Steven, who had finished their quick lunch. Steven still held a paper cup of coffee, which spilled part of its contents in the near collision.

"S-sorry!" stammered Jack, to whom even Sarah and Steven looked like imposing adults.

"No problem." Steven laughed. "It's terrible coffee!"

Jack ran on, and Sarah, taking Steven by the hand, started in the direction of Harvard.

"It really is awful coffee," she allowed. "The one point of theology on which all Quakers can agree is that Sunday coffee should be terrible."

"As a punishment for Quaker sins, no doubt," quipped Steven.

She made a face at him and said, "Quakers, at least, are assured of grace. Which is more than can be said of some people!"

Sarah's mind dwelt on the challenge Steven represented. She wondered, as they walked side by side, how long a relationship could last under the pressures of different religious faiths. She could not consider jettisoning Steven, things had gone too far for that. For the first time, Sarah found herself wondering what things would be like if she did become a Jew. Within a moment she dismissed the thought from her mind as impossible. She wondered if perhaps she should talk to her aunt Elizabeth about Steven.

Coming back out into the sunlight of the Meetinghouse yard, Adam sipped the bottom-of-the-pot coffee he had found for himself. He saw Tim sitting on the steps which led to a side door. The homeless man was in the midst of many other people but clearly alone. Adam gathered himself together and walked over to within two steps of Tim, squatted down so as to be at the same level, and said good morning. Tim nodded his head to indicate he had heard and continued to eat his sandwich.

"Well, it seems to be fall; it's getting cold again," said Adam, wishing he could think of something other than the weather to mention.

"Not bad yet," responded Tim.

For an instant, Adam tried to imagine what it might be like to be homeless and feel winter coming on. Quickly retreating from that unpleasant and frightening thought, he wondered what he and Tim might have in common. Adam knew that Tim felt unwelcome by most Quakers and he wished he could combat Tim's isolation.

"The Sox sure got romped on in the play-offs," ventured Adam, wondering if a homeless man might find things like the Red Sox frivolous.

Tim looked up, smiled briefly, and said, "That kid Brewer is overrated. He never wins the ones that count."

Relieved, Adam laughed and said, "They all looked silly last week throwing their ice chests out onto the A's field. Maybe they'll learn something from that and play some better ball."

"They could do OK if they let Peterson pitch; he's got an arm. And the team could sure use some better coachin' than what they've got." Tim paused and scratched his nose. "But there's always next year," he concluded. Saying this, he got up from the steps and moved away.

Adam said a soft, "See ya," and Tim walked slowly across the yard and into Longfellow Park. For a moment, Adam thought he saw John Hoffman coming from the park, but just then one of the Meeting's five-year-olds ran up to Adam, sloshing his coffee and demanding his attention.

Business Meeting began at one o'clock, in silence. Elizabeth Elliot let the silence grow and deepen for several minutes and then read a short passage from a Quaker writer of the eighteenth century concerning the need for simplicity in life. Because she was new to the job of Clerking, Elizabeth felt quite nervous about her choice of reading and her delivery. She paused for just a moment to collect herself, then introduced the assembled Friends to the agenda for the afternoon and called on Jane Thompson to give the first committee report on the activities of the Membership Committee. From there, the Meeting progressed to a brief report from the Building Committee and a rambling report from the First-day School Committee. No real action was required of the Meeting by any of these reports. The attentions of the community passed quickly on to the painful and divisive question of same-sex marriage.

The question of how to begin, or rather renew, discussion on the topic had been on Elizabeth's mind all morning. Quaker marriage had always been a separate issue from legal marriage, which the state controlled. Friends could therefore marry a widow to a widower in the normal Quaker way and if the couple did not get married in a courthouse, the woman could keep the Social Security benefits she was entitled to from her first husband. This clear distinction between the religious view of marriage and the legal view meant that Quakers could, if they wanted, marry anyone, including homosexuals. Although most members of the community supported same-sex marriage, a few, generally older, members were seriously alarmed at the prospect. In order to get the discussion off to a quiet beginning, Elizabeth called on an elderly but thoughtful and respected woman named Patience Silverstone and asked her to summarize what had gone before and put the question in perspective.

"We've spoken at length about issues surrounding homosexual life and the possibilities of homosexual marriage," began Patience. "The Meeting seems to feel clear about several things. We value and respect all our members. The Meeting approaches change cautiously, like any institution, but we feel change is possible, depending on where we are led. Opinions differ about same-sex relationships, in part because our members' experiences and ages differ so greatly.

"But so far we have thought about homosexual marriage in a vacuum. That may be a disservice to all concerned. Could we consider, for a moment, what it is we hope that heterosexual marriage can be? What is it in practice? Does our Meeting live up to its responsibilities toward the couples we have married over the past several decades?

"More than a few Quaker couples now get divorced. That was considered unthinkable for Quakers when I was young. Society in general has changed a lot, of course, but it's Quakers who permit Quaker divorce. We don't recognize divorce formally, but we remarry divorced Friends if they wish. And we do that despite the marriage vows we use that speak of lifelong commitment.

"In this compromised world, perhaps it's time Friends look carefully at what Quaker marriage has become. Heterosexual marriage, I mean. And we need to look at what our Meeting is doing, or failing to do, to uphold married life for those who choose it. It's in light of present reality that we should be speaking about same-sex marriage."

As always in such Meetings, silence was a part of the Quaker discussion. The room was quiet after Patience had spoken. After a couple of minutes, a young woman from the university rose and asked whether the word "marriage" should even be used by Quakers, since it carried with it the medieval connotations of property and subservience. Some older Friends glanced at one another, but none rose to oppose the idea which had been expressed. Elizabeth was sure more might be said on this point to her in private.

After longer or shorter intervals of silence, other Quakers spoke on different themes, but almost all were inclined to approve same-sex union as valid Quaker practice. Tom Redburn, an openly gay member of Meeting, spoke about the need for timely change in Quaker understanding and practices. His words implied that the Meeting should act now. He concluded by saying, "Friends, this question has been framed in unfortunate terms, at least from a gay perspective. The question is not about marriage. Quakers get married, right? At least that happens a lot of the time. The question is whether gays and lesbians can really be Quakers. If we can, then there is no problem. We simply participate fully in the life of the Meeting, becoming members, getting married or not, maybe raising kids, growing old, and then dying. Just like Quakers normally do. If we really are Friends, then Meeting life must be open to us. That's how I see the question."

Silence filled the Meetinghouse. No one spoke against what Tom had said. Absent from today's discussion was the hostility of earlier discussions on this subject, and Elizabeth began to wonder if the Meeting might reach unity on the question today.

John Hoffman rose from the same seat in which he had sat in worship earlier that day. As in the morning, he looked very intense and his voice was almost harsh as he spoke. He expressed himself in clear tones, however.

"As I see it, Friends, we have an important problem before us, and we should consider what is in our hearts, what has been standard practice in Quaker tradition, and what the Scriptures tell us about homosexuality. Clearly the emotions and ideas in our hearts are still conflicting. We have discussed this matter for over two years now, and we continue to find how different our attitudes are about gay and lesbian life. But Quaker tradition is clear. Quakers have married heterosexuals, and only heterosexuals. Part of what the word 'marriage' means to us is heterosexual life and the possibility of having children."

Looks of distress and pain passed over the faces of many. Patience Silverstone bowed her head. The silence was strained. John Hoffman took a breath and continued.

"And if Quaker tradition is not enough for us, then Christian Scripture should be. Paul is clear in what he writes in the first chapter of Romans: 'God has given them up to shameful passions. Their men, giving up natural relations with women, burn with lust for one another; males behave indecently with males, and are paid in their own persons the fitting wage of such perversion.' The Old Testament is clear about these matters, too. Leviticus tells us it is 'an abomination' for a man to lie with a man. Both in Scripture and in Quaker tradition, we cannot ignore God's voice. Homosexuality is not a taste like any other. It is contrary to God's will. This Friend cannot stand aside and let Cambridge Meeting proceed with the contemplation of marrying gays or lesbians."

Elizabeth's habitual half smile had disappeared long

before John had finished. She sighed and called for silence from all. As a lifelong Quaker she knew the verses John had used as well as he did. She wondered what John made of the Bible's report of Jonathan's deep love for David and Saul's effort to separate them. The Bible could be used in many ways. Elizabeth knew the Meeting needed much deep silence in order to progress.

Suddenly the stillness surrounding them erupted into sound. A large man ran to the center of the open floor space, looked around, and shouted, "Listen to me!"

Elizabeth recognized Tim even though he was turned away from her, the better to confront the group of Quakers sitting around on the benches. For a moment she was paralyzed and simply took in the scene.

"Listen! You hypocrites!" shouted Tim. "You talk about money! You talk about money? Look at all you have! And you call yourselves Friends of God!

"All of you are well off. And look at this fancy building you own! You talk about simplicity? About integrity? My God! And you, Hoffman, you're the worst. I know how rich you are. You think if you give us a little bit, we should be grateful. And that giving makes you a saint or something. Hypocrites like you! Jesus didn't live like you people. He wasn't a rich bastard. If you cared about Christian life, you'd listen to somebody like me, somebody who knows what it's like to have nothing."

By this point Adam Chrisler was by Tim's side. "Tim," he said, "we will listen to you, but we've got a Meeting going on here to decide some questions other than money matters." Adam put his hands in his pockets and stepped directly in front of Tim, looking him in the face. "Come outside and we can talk," he said gently.

Elizabeth recovered from her paralysis and considered

what she might do. She regretted that she had not spoken to Tim this morning. Clearly she had not done her job as Clerk. If she had talked with him, perhaps she would be able to understand better what was now going on. She remembered a couple of conversations with Tim in which he discussed the self-congratulatory tone of Quaker life and the problem of relative Quaker wealth in a neighborhood which included within it the poorest of Cambridge's poor. It was certainly true that middle-class Quakers suffered from hypocrisy and complacency; a homeless man, the Clerk had to admit, might see this more clearly than she.

Elizabeth slowly stood up and quietly said, "Tim, we do welcome you, but we need to be able to do our business in our own way. And at the moment we have another question before us, as important as the one you're bringing up."

Tim looked directly into the Clerk's face. "Don't you see the hypocrisy in all this?"

There was a pause filled with nothing but silence.

"Yes," said Elizabeth slowly, "I can see hypocrisy in all of us when I look for it. But I see sincere concern for our neighbors, too. I'm sorry if it doesn't always seem that way, but it's real, I think. And today we agreed to discuss a question that's important to everyone here, one we've been working on for years."

"Yeah, OK." Tim put his hands in his pockets and seemed to partially relax. "But he's the worst of all of you!" he said in a quieter tone and nodded at John Hoffman as he spoke. His face was still contorted with what seemed to be anger. Tim then turned, dodged around Adam, and strode out the door.

Elizabeth called for a return to silence. Adam followed Tim outside to see if he was all right and to fulfill his promise to listen if Tim still wanted to speak. Elizabeth went back to her seat. After so much strain, the Clerk was glad to slip into the comfort of prayer.

2

We utterly deny all outward wars and strife and fightings with outward weapons, for any end or under any pretence whatsoever. And this is our testimony to the whole world. The spirit of Christ, by which we are guided, is not changeable, so as once to command us from a thing as evil and again to move unto it; and we do certainly know, and so testify to the world, that the spirit of Christ, which leads us into all Truth, will never move us to fight any war against any man, neither for the kingdom of Christ, nor for the kingdoms of this world.

George Fox, 1661

Monday morning dawned dark and rainy. To the delight of schoolchildren and people who had the day off because of Columbus Day, the weather improved as the day progressed. By noon the sun came out and it washed greater Boston with warmth. New England in October can be beautiful, and the afternoon was gorgeous. The trees were just beginning to turn color, most birds had not flown south, and the air was clean after the rainstorm. Although the autumn equinox was past, the sun's rays reminded Bostonians that summer was as long a part of the year, even in New England, as winter.

The pace of the day was slower than most in the city, because of the semiholiday. The homeless were given a partial reprieve from their lot by the sun's warmth at noon. Tim, who had spent the night in Harvard Square and had slept badly, started the day in a foul mood. He spent the early morning dodging rain squalls and then bummed loose change from passersby. His take after two hours was small, only enough for coffee and a cinnamon roll. But as the sun came out at noon, his mood changed. He found a discarded *New York Times* and scanned the major stories. Then he walked toward Central Square, enjoying the sun. He was headed for a free lunch at the Salvation Army.

At the same time, Elizabeth Elliot left her home and went for a walk. She strolled to Fresh Pond, enjoying the sun and mild temperature. Lately she had been noticing how quickly the days were growing shorter. Elizabeth missed the long evening light of summer and was glad to spend some time in the midday sun. She returned home for a late lunch. Although she intended to write in her journal, she retired to an afternoon nap, promising herself more industry on the morrow. Her nap was ended in mid-afternoon by a telephone call from Patience Silverstone.

The elderly Quaker congratulated the Clerk on her conduct during the difficult Business Meeting of the previous day. Both Tim and John Hoffman had behaved in ways not conducive to Quaker decision making, said Patience, and the Clerk had handled the situation well.

Elizabeth thanked her lifelong friend for her words, and the two women discussed John Hoffman's statement opposing same-sex marriage. They agreed that such a strong denunciation of homosexual life was unexpected at this late date in the Meeting's discussions of the topic. But the Clerk must decide how to proceed from the current impasse. Elizabeth asked for Patience's support in prayer while she considered how to respond to John's statement.

Although in his sixties, John Hoffman did not stop for a nap. He felt deep and steady elation all morning. He stopped once or twice as he went about his work, simply to savor his inner peace and joy. His step as he moved about was light and his mind raced ahead, planning for the future. He hardly noticed the beautiful weather. His satisfaction with the day came from within, for his prayers had been answered.

John was taking the day off from work, putting his house to rights. He ate a large lunch and went into his backyard to survey his garden and contemplate what work was needed before winter. His garden had always been a joy to him and he looked across the faded roses with an almost fatherly concern for their well-being.

Columbus Day or not, good weather or bad, Bill Hoffman had to be at work early Monday. He now arrived at his darkened law office shortly after 7 A.M. At 3 P.M., he was finalizing the language of a contract he and one of his partners had been working on for weeks. He was glad to have the project off his back. As he put away his files on that client, he realized there were only a few minor things left on his desk. If he worked well, he said to himself, he could leave his office while there was still a bit of the late afternoon left to enjoy. Despite the fact that his mind was filled with images of himself in judicial robes, Bill worked efficiently. He alternated between seeing himself confirmed as a judge for the Commonwealth and applying himself to the more mundane tasks in front of him. An extremely able man, he did his work with dispatch in between moments of daydreaming.

At 4 P.M. the sun was low in the autumn sky. In Boston, outside city hall, Adam Chrisler held one end of a long cloth banner. The banner was one of many in a demonstration protesting the city's funding cuts in programs affecting the very poor. The afternoon's sunshine had been welcome to the protestors. The gathering was good spirited and peaceful, and Adam was glad to see the local TV news cameras setting up to tape the demonstration before the light faded.

In residential Cambridge, young Jack Nelson had spent the afternoon in rambunctious play. Enough leaves had fallen to provide him and his friends with material for entrenched fortifications in which "Iraqis" defended themselves against "Marines." Alice Nelson, unaware of exactly what the boys were playing, listened to their gleeful shouting and was happy that her boy was enjoying himself. At 5 P.M. Jack was called inside by his mother to watch *Square One* on television. At 6 P.M., as the sun set and darkness enveloped greater Boston, he was seated at the kitchen

table, happily eating spaghetti and meatballs, his favorite
supper.

Night brought quiet and rest to active people, and this
night was no exception. Midnight darkness found all members of the Quaker community, save two, safe in their beds.
Tim was curled up on a heating grate in Harvard Square,
sleeping as best he could, while John Hoffman lay dead in
his garden in Cambridge.

3

To consider mankind as other than brethren, to think favours are peculiar to one nation and exclude others, plainly supposes a darkness in the understanding. For as God's love is universal, so where the mind is sufficiently influenced by it, it begets a likeness of itself and the heart is enlarged toward all men.

John Woolman, 1754

The next day, at one o'clock in the afternoon, Elizabeth Elliot was having a cup of Darjeeling tea in the kitchen and looking at the *Boston Globe*. The kitchen was her favorite room. A cozy place, decorated in yellow tones, it felt warm even in the cold and dark months of New England's winter. The kitchen also had the virtue of being at the back of the house, and was thus sheltered from the worst of the Concord Avenue traffic noise. Elizabeth's backyard was small, but many years of faithful and year-round bird feeding had attracted a number of juncos and finches on an almost permanent basis. At home with the comforts of chirping birds and good tea, Elizabeth felt secure and at peace. Her husband had adopted a stray cat, whom he called Sparkle, shortly before his death. The cat still lived with Elizabeth, although it spent much of its life in the privacy of the basement and was never present in the main part of the house when Elizabeth had any company. But this morning the cat was curled up next to the radiator in the kitchen, and Elizabeth appreciated the company.

Nonetheless, it had been a sober morning. She had spent it making an entry in her journal and reading from John Woolman. Elizabeth often read Woolman. She felt insecure in her new role as Clerk of Meeting and hoped, as always, to find guidance and inspiration in the records of earlier Quakers. This morning her reading had concentrated on Woolman's choice of an economically simple life. She recollected what John Hoffman had said on Sunday about wealth and the Spirit. Elizabeth sympathized with the message and with Woolman's views on simplicity. She had always felt uncomfortable with her own middle-class life-style although she had never had the strength to change it. It was not a new problem for her, but this Tuesday morning she had the strength to examine her feelings and her life more deeply than usual.

Woolman had been an eighteenth-century Quaker in America, known for his deep spiritual calling and his opposition to slavery. He had traveled widely to oppose the slave trade at a time when most colonials and Englishmen accepted slavery as part of the natural order. Woolman wore plain, undyed clothes, rather than the finery of some Quakers of the time. He supported himself and his family in humble style. At length, he felt called to go to England to preach against the slave trade. English ships and English businessmen were at the heart of slavery, he felt, and he asked all who would listen to reconsider their trade in light of the gospel. While in England he contracted smallpox and died in 1772. Elizabeth had been taught to revere Woolman when she was a child and she still found his writings deeply moving.

For a moment Elizabeth paused to consider one of her more pressing financial decisions. Her 1977 Chevrolet, purchased used in 1980, was having increasing difficulties. Last winter it had stalled repeatedly when the motor was cold. Although Elizabeth had taken it to the garage more than once, the engine continued to sputter. During the summer the problem had gone away, but on cold mornings now she heard signs in the engine's voice that stalling would soon be a part of the daily routine when she used the car. Many small things about the car no longer worked. The gas gauge always read empty. It had done so since 1984. The right-rear door had been deeply creased while the car sat in the parking lot of the local Star market. The door could be opened and closed, but only with difficulty. And in the past several months, Elizabeth had been required to add a quart of oil every other time she filled it with gas. This, she knew, was not a sign of good things to come.

But she was on a fixed income. Pension money and Social Security checks supported her, but in modest style. By Woolman's eighteenth-century standards, of course, she was well off. But by modern Cambridge standards she was not. She hated the thought of tying herself to a new car purchase. It would require all she had. Given how infrequently she used her car, it did not seem right to purchase something so expensive. Quaker simplicity argued against the idea. Especially when the old car was running, even if it limped and lurched on occasion.

But now, after lunch, she was giving herself a break from serious thoughts about financial obligations and stewardship by looking at a Boston newspaper. The paper reported that yesterday, the Columbus Day holiday, the gubernatorial candidates were frantically busy as the November election neared. The Democratic primary in September had been won, to Elizabeth's horror, by a Boston academic, an angry "outsider" whom she thought was dangerously antidemocratic. Like most Quakers, Elizabeth was a lifelong Democrat and had been grieved by the primary. For the first time in her life, she was considering voting Republican. According to one of the *Globe*'s recent polls, many Massachusetts Democrats were having similar thoughts.

Additionally, the *Globe* reported a temporary disaster on the Red Line, the part of the subway linking Cambridge to Boston. Yesterday, at 3 P.M., a major gas leak had developed near the MIT stop. The Red Line had been taken out of service immediately. The gas leak had now been found; the paper reported that service would be restored today. Elizabeth wondered how the people who had to work on Columbus Day had gotten home from Boston. Bus service to and from the city center was infrequent compared to the subway. The *Globe* explained that buses had been on holiday schedule in honor of Christopher Columbus. It had apparently taken several hours for many workers to get out of Boston yesterday afternoon.

Sighing, Elizabeth put the newspaper aside. Her tea had grown cold. City life, she mused, had growing disadvantages. Yesterday she had almost gone downtown for the Columbus Day sales; now she was glad she had stayed at home, enjoying retirement.

Her mind turned to Quaker business. She wondered if she should summarize Sunday's Business Meeting for the monthly newsletter, a task that fell to her as Clerk. The job must be faced sometime, and Elizabeth began to collect her thoughts to address it. But she was interrupted by a telephone call from Jane Thompson, a longtime Meeting member.

Jane lived just two houses away from John Hoffman on Royal Avenue, located in a pricey neighborhood between Harvard Square and Fresh Pond. Jane was, like Elizabeth, a widow with grown children. Unlike Elizabeth, she took intense interest in all personal news of Meeting members. Elizabeth considered her to be a lonely woman, and perhaps because some days she could empathize with Jane's plight, she always felt a kind of irritation with her. Today was no exception, but Elizabeth listened through her annoyance.

"I saw several police cars and a police van at John's house this morning," said Jane. "Naturally, I went over to investigate." She was rather breathless. "John is dead. He was found in his backyard, in the roses there, by somebody or other."

Elizabeth's first thought was that a heart attack or stroke had claimed him as he had tended to the autumn chores of his rose garden, but Jane explained that a bystander she had spoken to had said John's head was "bashed in." Jane thought that Elizabeth, as Clerk of the Meeting, would want to know what had happened. Elizabeth was shaken by the news, but thanked Jane for calling. For once she was genuinely glad for her call. Jane hung up saying something about "those people" who were arriving in ever-increasing numbers in Cambridge. Elizabeth sighed and sat down once more at the kitchen table.

After some consideration, she called Bill Hoffman at his work number. A secretary answered and said, sounding efficient and almost cheerful, that due to an emergency in the family, Mr. Hoffman had gone home for the day. Elizabeth thanked her in what she hoped was a businesslike manner and declined to leave a message. She hung up and called Bill at his home. A tape recording of Bill's voice invited her to leave a message after the tone, which she did.

Because the telephone and the telephone book were before her, Elizabeth called Adam Chrisler. She had meant to call him on Monday to thank him for his help controlling the disruption Tim had caused, but she had not acted on her intentions. Now would be a good time to speak to him. Adam answered the phone immediately. His voice was quite hoarse and initially difficult for Elizabeth to recognize. But when she had said who she was and heard Adam's friendly response, she was sure she had the right number. She thanked him on behalf of the Meeting for his help with Tim on Sunday and added her own admiration for the compassion and poise with which he dealt with all the homeless people who found their way to Meeting. Adam said he was grateful for her words but undeserving of any praise. Elizabeth then mentioned that Jane Thompson had called to say that John Hoffman was dead. There was a pause before Adam responded.

"I'm sorry to hear that, of course," he said. "Do you know how he died?"

"I really know very little," said Elizabeth, "but I understand that the police are at his house."

"The police?" answered Adam. "I guess they always have to check out a sudden death."

Elizabeth wanted to ask Adam what he had made of John Hoffman's message Sunday morning. But this did not seem the right occasion for such a discussion. She and Adam said good-bye. Within a few minutes, Bill Hoffman called Elizabeth back.

"Jane Thompson called me earlier this afternoon," explained Elizabeth, "and I want to express my shock and sympathy about John's death."

"Thank you," said Bill, sounding grave but clearly glad to hear from her. "I'm afraid the situation is very distressing. My uncle was found this morning by his business partner, Erik Swensen. Erik was worried because Uncle John hadn't come into the office after the holiday yesterday and wasn't answering the telephone at home. He went to my uncle's house. It was locked up, so he walked around to the back and found him lying facedown in the rose garden. Apparently, he had been hit on the head. He was dead."

"Oh!" said Elizabeth. "How horrible! Who could do such a thing?"

"I wish I could say it was a burglar or something like that," replied Bill, "but the house had not been broken into and nothing on my uncle's person seems to be missing."

"What will the police do now?"

"I spoke to a Detective Burnham, who said he'll have to interview Uncle John's business connections and some Meeting people and, of course, me. I was his nearest relative, after all."

Elizabeth again expressed her sympathies and asked how she could be of help.

"We'll need to have a memorial service," said Bill wearily, "and I would hope you'd take charge of that. I'll have the body interred by the funeral-home people. A memorial Meeting could be anytime, maybe a couple of Saturdays from now."

Elizabeth assured Bill she would take charge. Normally, the Oversight Committee would have done so, but Elizabeth had been on that committee for many years and knew the procedures. As a lifelong friend of John, she wanted to help in any way she could. Elizabeth and Bill agreed to talk later about details. She hung up and prayed this tragic memorial might be the last while she was Clerk. She looked into her small backyard, watching the finches and recalling various committees she had served on with John Hoffman. Her mind began to drift back through the years.

Abruptly, the telephone rang again and, answering it, Elizabeth found herself speaking to Detective Stewart Burnham of the Cambridge police.

"I understand you're chairman of the Quaker Meeting, Mrs. Elliot," began the detective. "I have a few questions for you."

"Of course," said Elizabeth. She had the reservations any pacifist might have about the police, but she had always cooperated with the legal system. In the past, as a woman who put her energies mostly into being a wife and mother, her sheltered life had seldom led her to consider the difficulties of directly dealing with institutions like the police force. Now, as Clerk, she knew she must face things more squarely.

"What can I help you with?" she politely asked the detective.

"I'd like to know if there have been any problems in your

church that relate to Hoffman. If there were any personal difficulties, for example."

"None that I know of that would have provoked any violence," replied Elizabeth. "We always have discussions and disagreements in our Meeting, it's the way we make decisions. But nothing out of the ordinary has focused on John. I don't think the business of the Meeting can account for his death."

"That isn't quite what I heard from the man's nephew. He tells me there was a disturbance on Sunday involving Hoffman."

"Yes, that's true, but I'm sure that isn't connected with this," answered Elizabeth. "We've had a homeless man named Tim coming to our Meeting off and on for several years now. His speech is sometimes disconnected and sometimes aggressive, but he has never been an actual threat to anyone. I've seen Tim many, many times over the years and he's never been violent."

"Aggressive speech, as you call it," countered Burnham, "has been known to lead to violent actions."

"It might be convenient for Bill and us Quakers in general to think Tim responsible for whatever occurred at John Hoffman's house"—Elizabeth spoke with more spirit—"but Tim has been part of our community, in a way, for a long time now and I'm not afraid of him at all. It's certainly unfortunate that Tim was upset on Sunday. He may have seen what John said in our worship service as self-righteousness. Tim has spoken to me in the past about the callousness of middle-class Cambridge and the hypocrisy of various church groups, including our Meeting. But he's never been a danger to us over the years we've known him."

"That's your opinion, Mrs. Elliot, and I'll take it under

consideration, of course. But the fact remains that John Hoffman had no other enemies anyone knows about, he had no close family, no problems with his neighbors. On Sunday this man Tim threatened Hoffman and sometime on Monday Hoffman was killed. Obviously Tim is a good suspect. I've got orders out to pick him up for questioning."

"As Clerk of the Meeting, I'd appreciate knowing when you do find him. I'd like to speak to him while he's in your custody."

Detective Burnham coughed and said, "You have no right to speak to him, unless you're his lawyer."

"I know nothing about the law," answered Elizabeth, "but I'm his minister." Elizabeth, of course, had no claim to ordination, but all Quakers considered themselves to be ministers.

"OK, we'll inform you when we pick him up," responded Burnham, "but it's a matter of courtesy only. We're not required to do so."

"Thank you very much," answered Elizabeth. "I appreciate it. I repeat my offer to help you in any way I can. And of course the Meeting will cooperate with the police." She regretted her last sentence immediately.

"Good," said Burnham, "I'm sure we all want to see justice done. I'd like to know where Tim sleeps and if he comes to your church building during the week."

"During warm weather I've seen him sleeping on the grass of Longfellow Park, next to the Meetinghouse," answered Elizabeth. "I've never been entirely sure what he does at this time of year: it's certainly getting cold, but the shelters don't open until mid-November. He must find someplace more protected than the grass of the park to spend the night. During the week he's around, sometimes, as some of the other homeless are, but we've no meal for anyone except on Sundays.''

"Does he ever sleep inside your building?''

"We don't allow Tim or anyone else to sleep in the Meetinghouse. The Congregational and Lutheran churches in Harvard Square run homeless shelters, but we've never had the energy required to do so, I'm sorry to say.''

"Will you tell me if Tim shows up at your church in the next few days?'' asked the detective.

"Yes, I will. I'll tell him you're looking for him and advise him to call you, but I'll also tell you where and when I've seen him. I wonder if you might do me the favor of explaining a little bit of what has happened. John Hoffman was a longtime member of our Meeting, and I'd like to understand the circumstances of his death.''

"He was found in the backyard of his house,'' answered Detective Burnham. "I really can't say more than that while the investigation is underway, but we're certain there was foul play.''

"And do you know the time of his death?'' asked Elizabeth.

"I can't say, I'm afraid,'' said Burnham. "I'll get back to you if more questions about Tim or your Meeting come up. Meanwhile, I rely on you to let us know if Tim appears on your doorstep.''

Elizabeth said good-bye. She again fell into bird-watching out the back window, reviewing her conversation with Burnham and wondering what a Clerk's responsibilities were toward a man like Tim.

The telephone again brought her out of her musings. The call was from her niece Sarah Curtis. Elizabeth considered Sarah to be a good girl and she was always glad to hear from her. Although she occasionally saw Sarah across the Meetinghouse on Sunday mornings, they often did not say hello because of the press of Elizabeth's responsibilities as Clerk.

"It's always a pleasure to hear from you," began Elizabeth. "I've been wondering how things are going in school."

"Thanks. School is OK. Too much work, as usual, but I'm still enjoying the science classes. I'm taking a really great class in women's studies this semester. So I'm happy. But what I was wondering about just now was whether I could come by sometime, you know, and talk to you about my friend Steven."

"Certainly," answered Elizabeth smoothly although she was unsure who Steven was. "How about tomorrow evening?" she asked.

"Great! I'll come by after dinner at the house here, say about seven o'clock?"

"Fine," said Elizabeth. "We can have tea."

She turned away from the telephone, walking distractedly to the kitchen window. Her mind quickly left her niece and went back to what she knew of the Hoffman situation. She was sure that Tim was not involved, but also confident that both the police and many Quakers would find it easy to consider him guilty. In many ways, what the police did or did not do was not a concern of hers, but she did not wish Tim to be frightened or overwhelmed.

Elizabeth decided that she must talk to Tim. Perhaps he could establish his whereabouts and movements yesterday well enough to satisfy even a cynical policeman. She called a young man named Paul Stevens of the Meeting, an MIT student who volunteered at a homeless shelter run during the winter by the Lutheran Church in Harvard Square. He knew the details about shelters and soup kitchens and, she hoped, would understand where Tim spent most of his time during weekdays. She reached Paul in his dorm room and asked him where Tim might be.

"The days of the week are divided up among Harvard Square's soup kitchens so that we don't duplicate our efforts," answered the young man. "Today the supper meal is at Christ Church and tomorrow at St. Paul's. The shelters aren't open yet. We don't open until the middle of November, so your only bet is to try the soup kitchens. I'll keep an eye out for him, too."

"When does the meal at Christ Church begin?" asked Elizabeth.

"At five or five-thirty."

Elizabeth thanked the young Quaker and, looking at the clock, decided it was late enough to put on her coat and go to Christ Church. Buttoning up her navy wool coat, she locked her front door and went down her short sidewalk to Concord Avenue. She turned toward the Charles River and walked over the uneven brick sidewalks provided by the city of Cambridge.

The walk took her along the edge of Cambridge Common. The sun was low, and the scene was turning gray. Commuters were not yet cutting through the common on their way home; only the idle and displaced of Cambridge were there. She passed a dozen or so homeless people sitting and lying on the benches. One was feeding pigeons, but the rest seemed entirely unoccupied, having nothing to do but watch her pass. It surprised Elizabeth to see so many people here. Although some had sacks of belongings and sleeping bags, some appeared to have nothing at all. She wondered how anyone could survive being homeless once the New England winter descended. As she walked by the last homeless man lying down on a bench with his feet balanced on the edge of a trash can, she felt a sudden fear and a sense of disorientation. She was looking at the complete destitution of people she wanted to regard as neighbors. She repressed her fear and continued to walk at her normal pace. As she stepped into the crosswalk on Garden Street, she felt better, but she still had a vague sense of nausea from the common.

Christ Church was on the edge of Harvard Square. Elizabeth looked up at it as she crossed the street. The sanctuary predated the Revolutionary War. Indeed, a bullet hole from a skirmish between rebels and British Regulars could still be found in the front of the building, carefully preserved by the historically minded. Before the revolution, Christ Church had been part of the Church of England; after the colonies were severed from England, the congregation became Episcopalian. In modern times, the church had prospered. Its membership was now highly educated and well-to-do. Money was available to carefully refurbish and preserve the old sanctuary, which was open to tourists year-round. Students from Harvard's architecture classes came to Christ Church, as one of their first exercises of the year was to sketch the building and breathe in the form of an early New England structure, but there were no visitors in the gathering darkness.

Elizabeth headed to the building next to the sanctuary. It was recently built and not of historical importance, housing Sunday school classrooms, a room for choir practice, a large kitchen, a library, and a high-ceilinged hall. Elizabeth made her way to the hall where long tables were set up, each table surrounded by a dozen chairs. A few people were already seated at some of the tables, and the place was noisy. Elizabeth took off her hat and opened her coat. She looked around, thinking that there would be a din in this room when it became full. She asked an older man, clean and pleasant-looking, when the meal would begin.

"They're supposed to start serving at six o'clock, but sometimes they're late," he answered.

Elizabeth felt awkward and turned gratefully to a middle-aged woman who walked up and asked, "Are you here to volunteer?"

"Actually, I'm looking for someone, but I'd be glad to help until the meal is served," answered Elizabeth.

"OK, come with me. We can put your coat away and then put you to work in the kitchen. Who are you looking for? My name is Julia, by the way."

"Thank you. I'm Elizabeth Elliot and I'm looking for a fairly big man named Tim. He's young, at least by my standards, and he's been around Harvard Square for several years now."

"I think I know Tim," answered Julia, "the big guy who's smart but a little unpredictable?"

"Yes," said Elizabeth, "that's him."

"He comes here most weeks. I can keep an eye open for him tonight, if you'd like."

Elizabeth thanked her and went to work chopping vegetables under the direction of a volunteer who, it turned out, was a Boston University graduate student and had once come to Friends Meeting as a visitor. Elizabeth and the student chatted as they worked until, just before six o'clock, Julia returned and said, "Tim has just come in. He's at the back table."

Elizabeth thanked her, excused herself from the kitchen work, dried her hands, and went out into the hall. She spotted Tim quickly. He looked more disheveled than usual and was glancing all around the hall. He took a cigarette out of his shirt pocket and lit it as Elizabeth approached.

"May I sit here?" she inquired, indicating the chair across the table from Tim.

Tim shrugged his shoulders and looked away. Then he turned to her with a puzzled expression on his face and said, "I didn't know you volunteered for Episcopals."

"No," answered Elizabeth, "I don't. I came here tonight to look for you because I'm afraid of things that are happening. I'm Clerk of Friends Meeting and I feel responsible for what happens around our community. You're part of that community."

"I still don't get it," said Tim. He inhaled his cigarette. "Why are you at this holy, catholic, and apostolic church?"

"I'm worried about you because of John Hoffman's death yesterday."

"Hoffman is dead? I didn't know that." Tim seemed confused. "He was old. Did he just die?"

"No. He was killed by someone. He had been hit on the head very hard, it seems," replied Elizabeth.

"Really!" exclaimed Tim. "I'm sorry. He was a pompous old guy, but he was good to me."

"Did you know him, then?" asked Elizabeth. It was now her turn to be puzzled. She had certainly never seen Tim and the respectable John Hoffman speaking to each other at Meeting.

"Sure, I knew him! Had for a long time! And I talked to him just recently and went to his house. It's hard to imagine that he's dead. We walked together to Royal Avenue on Sunday, after that Business Meeting of yours," answered Tim.

Startled, Elizabeth considered this.

"John Hoffman and me did OK together," continued

Tim. "I sometimes walked home with him after Meeting and if he had heavy stuff to move in that garden of his, I'd haul it for him. He always gave me ten bucks, and that's good where I come from. The work never took that long. Once in the summer I watered the lawn and the roses while he was out of town. Did it for two weeks. He didn't give me the key to his house, you understand, but he was glad for the help, I could tell."

Abruptly, Tim rose from the table and went to the back of the hall. Now that she looked, Elizabeth could see a coffeepot there. She had not noticed it before. She wondered if Tim would return or if he considered this conversation at an end. After getting a cup of coffee and stirring in five spoons of sugar, Tim turned, walked back to the table, and pulled up a chair once more.

"It's always bad coffee here," he said.

Elizabeth seized the subject. "It's always awful coffee at the Meetinghouse."

"Sure is!" said Tim with a brief smile.

"Tim," said Elizabeth more seriously, "a lot of Quakers wonder about you. Because of the things you said about John Hoffman on Sunday and the way you said them. John is dead and you may be suspected of harming him."

"I don't give a shit what people think," said Tim, and looked away from Elizabeth.

"Neither do I," she said, "but I care what the police think. It seems that John was killed on Monday. Where were you yesterday and how can we prove it to the police?"

"I don't have to say nothin' to the police. I know my rights." Tim paused and ground out his cigarette. Then he sipped his coffee. "But since you've come here and all, I'll tell you where I was. I slept beside Holyoke Center on the heating grate, there in Harvard Square, like usual. And I spent the morning bumming change from the subway rid-ers right here on the Red Line. Monday lunch they give us down at the Salvation Army in Central Square. That's where I was at about one o'clock. I stayed there after lunch and got a shower and this shirt and sweater too, 'cause that's where they give them out. You Quakers have lots of clothes in your Meeting's basement, I know, but you never give them out."

"Not often," said Elizabeth. "I don't know, maybe we should. But they're shipped to Philadelphia and distributed from there."

"That doesn't make sense if you ask me," said Tim.

For a moment it made no sense to Elizabeth either, but she put aside the thought and asked, "When did you leave the Salvation Army building?"

"Not until six," said Tim. "The guy there made a mistake. After I took a shower he thought I left since everybody else was gone. Anyway, he wandered away, so I pulled out some of the old clothes from the bin in the dressing room, made me a little bed on the floor, and slept like I was dead. At six the same guy came in to turn off the lights and stuff, and he threw me out."

Elizabeth sighed and relaxed a little bit backward in her chair. To make sure of Tim's story she or the police should check with the volunteers at the Salvation Army. Clearly no one could testify to his whereabouts during the morning when Tim said he had been in Harvard Square, unless passersby would come forward to say they had given him change.

"Tim, you have to call the police. Ask for a Detective Burnham. Because of what you said about John on Sunday they're wondering if you killed him. The best thing to do is go in and talk to them and explain just what you did, as you did to me."

"It's crazy to think I would kill Hoffman or anybody else.

I'm not going to call them. They can come to me if they want to talk."

Elizabeth could see no way of changing his mind. She knew Tim to be a determined and stubborn man.

"OK," she said. "But if you change your mind, please remember Burnham's name. By the way, do you know the name of the man you mentioned at the Salvation Army?" asked Elizabeth.

"No. I don't like the army people, so I never learn their names," answered Tim. "You Quakers are better about not preaching at the homeless like the army does." He paused and then began in an angrier tone of voice. "But the army people at least live with us. They live poor, and they know what it's like to have nothin'."

Pained, Elizabeth did not know how to respond. She waited a minute but did not see how she could usefully speak further to Tim tonight. So she wished him a good evening, rose, and left the table. As she got her navy-blue coat, it suddenly seemed ostentatious and unnecessarily fine. It was a good coat, but she had purchased it on sale in Filene's basement the previous spring. Surely, thought Elizabeth, it is nothing to be ashamed of. As she left, supper was being served in the kitchen and carried out to the working poor, the elderly, and the homeless who had gathered. The room was indeed as noisy as she had expected and was already filled with tobacco smoke. Elizabeth went out the side door of Christ Church and into the cleaner air of the cold evening. Rush hour was still underway as she walked away from the square back up Concord Avenue. It would certainly frost this night, and Elizabeth wondered where Tim would sleep if the police did not pick him up early in the evening.

When Elizabeth got home, she called the Cambridge

police and left a message for Detective Burnham saying that she had seen Tim at Christ Church at dinnertime. She took a dose of her blood pressure medicine and then prepared her own supper, more grateful than usual for her clean and quiet kitchen.

4

[The struggle for salvation] began for most [seventeenth-century] Friends with a hard, slow, inner conflict; only afterward could they call themselves the children of the Light. This opening struggle shaped the meaning of their new lives and gave color to all they thought or felt about the inward Light. . . . The end of it was peace and joy, a sense of conquering kingdoms and demons, and a deep unity of love with other Quakers. The serenity and trust and the sense of daily direction from the Spirit finally became the most characteristic part of the Quaker way of life.

Hugh Barbour, 1964

The *Boston Globe* for Wednesday reported John Hoffman's murder in a story on page 8. Elizabeth Elliot read it carefully, but it contained no more information than Burnham had been willing to tell her over the phone. She was on her second cup of tea and midway through her written summary of the previous Sunday's Business Meeting when she received a telephone call from Hugo Coleman of the Finance Committee of Quaker Meeting. Hugo was a widower of Elizabeth's age, and in the past year a certain tension had developed between them. Hugo often invited Elizabeth to social events, but Elizabeth always declined. The invitations were then repeated. Elizabeth always strove to be friendly with people, especially Quakers, and this was apparently misinterpreted by Hugo. Happily for both Elizabeth and Hugo, he did not have socializing on his mind today.

Hugo explained that he was concerned that John Hoffman's pledge to the Meeting, which made up a sizable fraction of the budget and which was always paid at the end of the calendar year, would not now come in. The Finance Committee had been counting on John's donation in December. Without it, the group would fall farther behind than usual in its budget for this fiscal year.

"But I was wondering," said Hugo, "if you might know whether John left money to us in his will."

"I wouldn't be surprised," responded Elizabeth, "but I certainly don't know one way or the other. Bill Hoffman always acted as his lawyer and I'm sure Bill will tell us when it's appropriate."

"Yes, but meanwhile the Finance Committee has to try to keep this Meeting solvent. We put in a new furnace in September. There was no choice about that, and now the bill has come due. We are blessed with an endowment, of course, but none of us wish to use it for operating expenses."

"I'm sure the membership will rise to the occasion," said Elizabeth, grateful she was not on the Finance Committee. Fortunately, the Cambridge Quaker Meeting was large enough so that the Clerk did not have responsibility for money questions. All cash-flow concerns fell to Hugo and others on the Finance Committee, a committee to which Elizabeth had never belonged. Although she had often thought the Meeting depended too much on Hoffman money, both John's and Bill's, especially when a building project or a big bill came in, she had never had to face the realities of the group's cash flow. Looking back on her years of service, she realized she had done only the traditional "women's work" of Sunday school teaching and coffee making. Although those things were important, she was beginning to realize that as Clerk she had accepted responsibilities that were new to her. But the details of finances were certainly not her first priority.

Hugo said he might tactfully ask Bill Hoffman about his uncle's will. "It's crucial to the Meeting, after all, and although I'm sure he's deeply grieved by his uncle's death, I trust Bill won't be upset by my asking. He's a lawyer, after all, and he knows that these sorts of things are important. We have to plan. The Meeting has to know where it stands. But I'll be gentle when I inquire and, of course, express my sympathy."

Elizabeth could not see a polite way of forestalling Hugo; he was clearly set upon a course she did not like, but she did not have the energy at the present to argue with him. She made a noncommittal remark, then mentioned she must get back to a matter that was pressing her, and so the conversation ended.

Hugo's call reminded Elizabeth to telephone Erik Swensen, John Hoffman's business partner in his real estate firm. She looked up Swensen's number and reached him at his business. She expressed her sorrow at his partner's death.

"I'm calling to assure you that when we have a memorial Meeting for John, we would welcome your presence," said Elizabeth.

Erik Swensen thanked her and said he wished to come. He also said he had something which John had written long ago, in the early days of their partnership, which would be appropriate for someone to read and he volunteered to do this himself if that was agreeable. Elizabeth explained briefly that Quakers did not read any materials, not even Scripture, at memorials or any other Meeting. Quaker silence was meant as a time to listen, not speak, unless spontaneously led to do so by the Spirit. Erik did not seem to grasp what she meant. He mumbled something about not wishing to do anything extraordinary, only show John in his best light. She made a mental note to speak to Erik again about this shortly before the event, since Quaker silence sometimes led outsiders to believe that their readings or speech making would be perfectly welcome.

"I understand you found John," said Elizabeth.

"Yes," answered Swensen. "He didn't come into work and wasn't answering the telephone. It wasn't like John to neglect our work, and since Monday had been a holiday, there was a lot to do. By eleven I was worried enough to go to his house. The front door was locked and he didn't answer the doorbell, so I went around back to see what I could. I don't know why I went into the rose garden, exactly, but when I did I saw him there."

"It must've been a great shock to you," said Elizabeth.

"Yes. There was a lot of blood on his head."

"Were you sure right away he was dead?"

"Yes, I knelt down and felt him. He was cold, so there was no doubt about it. I hadn't seen a corpse since my days in the army, but I knew he was dead."

"It certainly must've been traumatic, Mr. Swensen. I do hope this won't end your business enterprises, although I'm sure it must disrupt everything. I don't know how the partnership law works when one partner dies."

"I don't think it will end everything. We went to a lawyer years ago and set things up so that John's estate will continue to get his share of the profits, but I won't have to buy out his share as long as the business is running. That's pretty standard in partnerships. John really cared about this business, and I'm sure he'd want me to keep going with it."

"I'm sure he did," said Elizabeth, "although I gather there had been some changes in his views recently concerning business life and money matters. Do you know anything about that?"

"I don't know what you mean, Mrs. Elliot."

"From something he said on Sunday I thought perhaps he was leaving business life," said Elizabeth, distressed that she was breaking Quaker protocol by referring to a message from worship in this way.

"That's news to me. I'm sure that John would have talked to me before he considered any major changes. I know neither one of us was interested in retirement, at least not soon."

Elizabeth closed the conversation by again expressing her sorrow and assuring Erik she would keep in touch with him about the memorial Meeting. She hung up the telephone and sat down at the kitchen table. She wondered what John Hoffman had been thinking about. Could sudden changes late in life lead to anything good in this world? Perhaps John's new will, if he had written one out before his death on Monday, would show what his new priorities had been. But certainly it seemed to Elizabeth that John might have done a better job keeping his colleagues and his friends informed about what was happening. People depended on him, after all. That thought reminded Elizabeth of Tim; she wondered if the police had found him yet. She shook her head as her feeling of confusion mounted, then stood up and took out her recipe book and began baking her week's bread. Her arthritis was not bad at the moment, and she wanted to use her hands. She mixed a batch of rye dough and kneaded it well. Setting it to rise on top of the stove, she realized she needed to take some sort of direct action about the Hoffman situation. Leaving the kitchen a mess, she prepared to leave the house.

Five minutes later, in her navy-blue coat and carrying an umbrella in honor of the threatening clouds, Elizabeth walked up Royal Avenue toward Hoffman's house. She walked more quickly when she neared Jane Thompson's. It looked quiet, and in view of the threatening rain, Elizabeth hoped that Jane would not decide to come out. Unlike Jane, Elizabeth did not assume that "outsiders" were responsible for violence in Cambridge. She knew good Quaker pacifists with violent tempers and other Quakers who could rationalize almost any action. She did not automatically blame people outside of Meeting for all the wrong done in the world. And especially not all the wrong done in a quiet and wealthy neighborhood like Royal Avenue. But she was uncomfortable with herself, in some ways, for wanting to see the scene of the crime. It was, after all, police business. Was there anything which Quaker methods of decision making or Quaker prayer could usefully address when it came to investigating a murder? On the other hand, she thought, a member of her Meeting had been killed, and killed while she was Clerk. It was an extraordinary happening and it pulled her toward John Hoffman's house. A certain horror was in her, but also a sense of responsibility which she could not clearly define. She recognized she was out of her depth, and she would be glad to turn her feelings of responsibility over to the police after seeing Hoffman's yard.

As she walked, Elizabeth considered what she knew about this murder. If the victim had been working in his rose garden, it would have been during daylight hours. At this time of the year that meant some time before about 6 P.M. Since he had apparently taken Columbus Day off from work, he could have been murdered anytime during the day up until the very end of the afternoon. Had the police already been able to narrow the time more than that?

Reaching the house, she saw that it was dark and quiet. As she had hoped, the police had taken whatever they felt they needed from the scene of the crime and departed. Nothing in the front or side yards was cordoned off, perhaps because the police believed they had found any physical evidence there was and had nothing to fear from neighborhood children or snoops.

Elizabeth walked up to the front door and rang the bell. There was no answer.

"Perhaps Bill is here in the backyard," she said, thus justifying, to some small degree, walking around the west side of the house to the back.

Elizabeth had been to this house for Quaker business of one sort or another through many years, but she was more familiar with the interior than with the yard. To her surprise, the yard was wide and deep behind the house, unusual for Cambridge. In the center stood a large island of rosebushes with a brick path through their midst. She thought there must be fifty bushes growing within it. The bushes were not pruned for winter. A few had new mulch spread around them. Perhaps it was that task at which John had been working on Monday afternoon. She brushed a few raindrops from her glasses and put up her umbrella. The dull rosebushes looked elegant and grim, not unlike all of New England in the autumn.

The grass grew wetter as Elizabeth circled the rose-bushes. She saw nothing but a few leaves blown in from neighboring yards. Then a squirrel scampered down the walk. She circled the center of the yard and returned to where she had begun. Next she walked down the brick path into the garden and saw, to her left, a place where several rosebushes had been crushed to the ground. This must have been where John had fallen. There were several broken-down bushes. Unless the police had injured the roses while doing their work, then someone else besides John had fallen here.

Elizabeth was confident the police had carefully searched the area and because the rain was falling harder every minute it certainly made sense for her to abandon this vaguely defined visit. But she lingered a little, looking at the mud, the bushes, and the edge of the brick walkway. Water began to run down the gentle incline of the bricks and in a minute a small stream would form. Elizabeth stooped over to knock mud from her boot. As she did, she saw something small and bright glisten as rain washed mud from it. While she looked, a little more water flowed across the bright object, exposing a gold cross in the wet earth. She picked it up and found it was attached to a thin gold chain, now broken. The chain had been invisible down amidst the mud clods and was coated with dirt.

She washed both the cross and the chain off in a puddle of rainwater forming on the bricks. As she stood in the rain, looking at the crucifix, she felt vague unease at such high church symbolism, but she also felt awe and respect for the ultimate sacrifice of innocence. With a shock of recognition, she realized that Tim, innocent though he was, could easily be sacrificed to what this garden had seen.

Elizabeth wondered what an icon, a gold one at that, could be doing in the yard of such a staid old Quaker as John Hoffman. Members of the Society of Friends normally did not own anything like crosses. Such things were thought popish or superstitious. Still, in these sad days of laissez-faire Quakerism, truly anything was possible. It could be that a number of the younger people in Meeting would think nothing of an icon around their necks. She was also afraid, however, that the crucifix was the type of thing Tim might wear. She certainly remembered his wearing a rather large and showy ring at one time. Elizabeth pocketed her find and turned to walk home. She was not sure what her duties toward the police might be at this point, duties dictated by the law and by her conscience. She chose not to think carefully about them. Quaker tradition gives no clear answers on questions concerning the law, nor indeed on some questions concerning moral obligations. It promises only that those who pray may be led to God's will. She found an old song running through her head called "Standing in the Need of Prayer." Elizabeth Elliot realized she had much prayer ahead of her. She trusted that Quaker silence could lead her forward.

5

Learning to live contentedly without high consumption goes against the grain of our culture, but is possible in the context of the community. Incomes can be cut if every family does not have to have its own laundry facilities, tools, automobiles, houses, etc. Concern for the ecosystem adds to the need for developing a simple yet adequate life style. Simplifying our lives also means pruning our scatter of activities to focus energy and to provide time to be present to each other.

American Friends Service Committee, 1975

Because she decided to stop by the Meetinghouse, Elizabeth did not walk directly to her home. Traffic was thickening on Huron Avenue as she turned toward Longfellow Park. Heavy traffic and crime were not new to a city like Cambridge, of course, but both still felt new to Elizabeth, even though she had lived in this neighborhood all her life. Crossing the heavy traffic on Brattle Street, she stepped into the relative quiet of Longfellow Park and breathed more freely. She walked into the Meetinghouse, pausing long enough at the door to put down her wet umbrella and hang up her coat. The ever-present musty odor of the building was strong today because of the rain. Elizabeth wondered if the odor would be gone when the old cork floor was removed, as the Building Committee was proposing. Since she associated the heavy, varnishlike smell with Quaker life, she would be a little sorry to lose it.

Elizabeth needed to check the Clerk's mailbox. There was always a lot of correspondence for her. Friends felt free to request the Clerk's opinion on questions ranging from aid to illegal refugees from El Salvador to the possibility of the Meeting printing tasteful Quaker Christmas cards for its membership. Elizabeth picked up her mail, sorted through it to make sure no great disasters were crashing down upon Quakerdom, and then stopped to chat with Harriet Parker, the secretary of the Meeting.

"Good morning, Friend," said Elizabeth. "I hope you are well." Both women had been members of Cambridge Friends Meeting for several decades and often worked together on committees. Harriet respected Elizabeth's judgment and her generosity toward the Quaker community down through the years. Elizabeth, for her part, truly admired Harriet for her serious education. Harriet had earned an M.A. in classics at Harvard in the 1950s, a rare

accomplishment for any woman at that time. She had declined teaching work to devote her energies to what Quakers needed.

"Hello, Elizabeth," said Harriet, looking up from the
papers on her desk and returning a smile. "Yes, I'm well,
thank you. Have you heard the sad news about John
Hoffman?"

"Yes, it's very shocking," answered Elizabeth in a lower
tone. "On Sunday we all saw John, but now he's taken away
from us. Except in spirit, of course."

"I saw him on Sunday," said Harriet, "and I spoke to
him on the telephone on Monday afternoon about the
newsletter for next month. It's difficult for me to grasp that
he was killed that same day!"

Elizabeth looked intently at Harriet and asked her at
what time she had spoken to John.

"Well, let's see. I'd been out for coffee in Harvard
Square. It was Columbus Day and I didn't really have to
come in at all, but since we were behind on the newsletter
I decided to put in some time. I had coffee with an old
school friend and came here about four o'clock. I called
John's work number but there was no answer, so I tried him
at home and reached him there."

"So you spoke to him shortly after four P.M.?" asked
Elizabeth, already feeling relief for Tim, who had a good
chance of establishing his whereabouts in the late afternoon.

"Yes," said Harriet. "I remembered what he had said in
worship on Sunday morning, and after we talked about the
newsletter, I asked in a general sort of way how things were
at his business. He laughed and said it was fine, as far as he
knew, but that his days as a businessman were almost over.
He said something about wanting to spend more time

watching his roses and living quite differently. But it seemed that he really didn't want to say more about it, at least not to me. I wanted to talk to him about what he'd said in the afternoon at the Meeting for Business, but I felt awkward about it somehow. As I think you know, I myself am a little uncomfortable with the speed the Meeting is approving same-sex marriage."

"Yes," observed Elizabeth, "we've been discussing it for only two years." She waited to see if Harriet would respond to her mild sarcasm. Harriet, a good Quaker but a Puritan in temperament, pretended she had not heard.

"I appreciated part of John's message against such marriages," continued Harriet. "I'm not saying I'm truly opposed, because I'm not, and I surely won't stand in the way of any decision the Meeting makes. But I think it is good we move slowly, Elizabeth, something some of the younger Friends don't seem to appreciate. I wasn't sure how to say anything about that to John, though, since I've always thought his nephew is gay, and I'm not sure John knows that or would like to talk to me about it. And of course Bill was sitting right there in the Meeting for Business when John said that homosexual life was against God's will. Anyway, I didn't know how to discuss it, so that was the end of our conversation."

"It might be a good thing to write down what you just said to me about the time of this telephone call, Harriet, in case the police ask you later. By the way, Bill has asked me to take charge of organizing the memorial Meeting for his uncle. Can you tell me what groups are using the Meetinghouse for the next several Saturdays?"

Harriet turned to get the calendar and the two women looked over the schedule of racial awareness, antipoverty, environmental, and pacifist workshops that were already set down. The Saturday two weekends hence was clear in the afternoon and Elizabeth reserved that for a Meeting for Worship to celebrate the life of John T. Hoffman. After asking Harriet to clear the date with the Oversight Committee and then put a sign up on the bulletin board announcing the memorial, Elizabeth, gathering up her mail, said good-bye. She retrieved her coat and umbrella and went out into a light rain. She walked up Concord Avenue and returned to her home.

The rye bread dough, left to its own devices for too long a time, was almost overflowing the bowl. Elizabeth had put it on the center of the stove when she had left, and the warmth of the pilot light had done more work than she had anticipated. She washed her hands and then punched down the dough. She formed it into round loaves, put them on greased cookie sheets, and set them on the cool counter to rise more slowly. She covered the dough with damp tea towels, clean from the drawer, and felt satisfied with her progress as a baker.

Elizabeth called Detective Burnham from the kitchen to tell him of her visit to John Hoffman's house and her discovery of the gold cross. She expected she might encounter some hostility from the detective for snooping around. She had to admit she would never have told the police, or anyone else, that she had been to John's backyard if it were not for her discovery there.

Burnham answered his telephone promptly, and before Elizabeth could begin her explanation, he began to speak. "I know you called last night to say where Tim Schouweiler had eaten supper," he said defensively. "Thanks for that. One of our officers picked him up later in the evening; he was going to sleep on one of the heating grates at Holyoke Center in Harvard Square. We're holding him here in Central Square. I was going to call you about this; it's been a busy morning and I just haven't got to it yet. If you want to speak to him," continued Burnham with a little more confidence, "you can come down here right now."

"Yes, thank you," answered Elizabeth quickly. "I'll do that." She was glad to postpone her part of the conversation, and she did want to see Tim. The bread presented a problem, however. It would rise far too much while Elizabeth was away. Now that it had been formed into loaves, it did not require much time to rise, even away from the pilot light. After a moment's thought, she put the loaves back into the big bowl in which they had come to life, put all the damp tea towels on top of the mound, and put the bowl into the fridge. This required moving the milk, the orange juice, and the ketchup, but she was confident the work was worthwhile. The rye dough would stay sluggish in the fridge until she returned to let it grow again.

Elizabeth put on her coat and hat, called good-bye to Sparkle on the spur of the moment, and went out her front door. She walked down Concord Avenue, through the common to Harvard Square, and took the Red Line for the short trip to Central Square. She found her way to the police station, which she had never been inside, and asked at the front desk for directions to Burnham's office. The detective turned out to be a big man with a large and open face. There was no friendliness in his tone or manner as he greeted Elizabeth. He was well dressed in a white shirt, dark tie, and gray suit. He reminded her of a New England banker.

"Thank you for inviting me down here," she began. "There are a couple of things I happen to know now that I think you should be aware of."

"Oh, really?" answered the detective, motioning for Elizabeth to sit down. "What are they?"

"Last night I went to the soup kitchen at Christ Church, and Tim and I spoke to each other. He had not heard of John Hoffman's death, it seemed, and when I asked him if he would tell me where he was on Monday he answered openly with no hesitation. Have you asked him about his activities on Monday?"

"Yes, we've asked him a number of things, actually, but he won't answer. We've asked if he wants a lawyer present but he says no, he just won't talk to us. Right now we're holding him on vagrancy, but soon we may upgrade that to a murder charge."

"That would be a mistake, Mr. Burnham. Tim is no killer. And he knew and liked John," answered Elizabeth. "He worked a little for him, raking leaves and such, and he has taken care of the garden at least once when John was out of town."

"Mrs. Elliot, you are wonderful," said Burnham. "I haven't been able to get anything out of Schouweiler! So he knew the victim well enough to have been around his house over quite a period of time. That fits. On Sunday he spoke angrily against Hoffman, and on Monday Hoffman was killed in his garden. It all starts to look more and more probable."

"No, Mr. Burnham, I'm sure that's the wrong track," answered Elizabeth firmly. "He was ignorant of John's death until I told him what had happened. He was quite open in telling me he had worked for John in the past, and surely he wouldn't do that if he were guilty. Tim is a different sort, but nothing he said to me last night makes me believe he's killed anyone."

"I'm sure you believe that, Mrs. Elliot, but someone did kill Hoffman. A nice lady like yourself doesn't want to believe that anyone could be a murderer, but someone is.

And it's obvious to me that Tim Schouweiler could well be the man."

"I didn't know Tim's last name, by the way," said Elizabeth, "and I am sure no one at Meeting does either. If he voluntarily told you his name, I hope you can see he is cooperative, in his own way. But whatever you may think, please listen while I tell you where Tim was on Monday."

"I'll listen, Mrs. Elliot, but don't expect me to believe everything you do," replied the detective.

"Tim slept in Harvard Square on Sunday night," began Elizabeth, "perhaps at the same place you found him last night. At any rate, in the morning he panhandled in Harvard Square, in the subway area mostly, I think. At one P.M. he came down here to Central Square to the Salvation Army where there's a lunch. He got a shower and some new clothes after lunch."

Burnham was looking skeptically at a point over her left shoulder.

"You can check all of this out with the Salvation Army people," said Elizabeth quickly. "By chance he was left alone in their clothing room there and he says he curled up on some clothes and slept all afternoon. You can check this because at six o'clock one of the men who worked there found him in this room, where he apparently should not have been allowed to stay, and got him to leave.

"John Hoffman was alive at four P.M.," continued Elizabeth. "He was still at work in his garden when the murderer came to his house. That must have been before six P.M., when it would be too dark to work. So Tim is innocent: from four to six o'clock he was asleep inside the Salvation Army building in Central Square, almost two miles away from Royal Avenue."

"He may have been found there at six, but that certainly

doesn't prove where he was at four or five o'clock, Mrs. Elliot. Don't you see, he might say anything at this point to mislead you. Why, by the way, do you think Hoffman was alive at four?"

"I know he was alive at four P.M. because Harriet Parker, our church secretary, spoke to him on the telephone at that time."

"I didn't know that. Once again, I'm glad for the information," responded Burnham. He quizzed Elizabeth about her conversation with Harriet and took down her name and the Meeting's telephone number. "I'll check with her and take a statement," he said. "But Tim Schouweiler is still our number one suspect no matter what he may say about sleeping the afternoon away. You know it may partly be true: he may have been drunk, killed Hoffman because he was angry with him, and then gone to sleep the way drunks do, maybe in the Salvation Army like he says."

Elizabeth, guarding against showing her exasperation, repeated her request that the police interview the gentlemen who worked at the Salvation Army. There seemed little else to say, however, so she asked if she might speak to Tim. The detective rose and motioned her out of his office door.

He showed her to a visitors' room. He disappeared, but soon brought the prisoner. Tim was dressed in what were apparently jail clothes: a gray jumpsuit made of cotton and no sweater. Elizabeth hoped the cells were well heated. Perhaps for an old building in New England that was a lot to hope. Elizabeth made a mental note to ask Tim if he needed anything warmer to wear. He looked tired and passive. Elizabeth wondered at the speed with which jail was affecting him.

Burnham sat Tim down on a chair and left them, saying, "I'll be back in ten minutes, Mrs. Elliot. You just holler if he causes you trouble. There's a man just down the hallway."

"I'm sorry about that, Tim," began Elizabeth. "I came to see how you were and if there is anything I can do."

"I can't see how," said Tim. "The motherfuckers here won't let me out at least until the preliminary hearing is over. That's gonna be in a couple of hours they say."

"Did you tell them where you were on Monday afternoon?" asked Elizabeth.

"No, I don't talk to cops. I don't say nothin'," answered Tim.

Again, Elizabeth fought her exasperation. Men, in her opinion, had natural tendencies toward pigheadedness which women only rarely matched. Both Tim and Burnham were trying her patience. She could see who would have to speak on Tim's behalf. She felt the small gold cross, still in her coat pocket. If she was going to give this to the police she might as well give Tim some warning about it. Elizabeth did not know if she were doing the right thing, but she had only a little time to think. With a small prayer, she drew out the cross in her thin and delicate hand. She opened her palm to show the crucifix and asked, "Tim, is this yours by any chance?"

Tim looked at her hand with a blank expression, then brightened up and said, "Thank you! Where did you find it?"

He took it from Elizabeth with both of his thickened and dirty hands. Looking at it, he said, "The chain's broken. That must be why I lost it. Where did you find it?"

Elizabeth, whose heart had sunk but was now recovering as she looked at Tim's smiling face, answered him briefly, saying that she had found it in John Hoffman's rose garden.

Tim, unconcerned by that information, was tying the chain together. "I'm glad to have this back," he said. "Last spring I looked all around for it, but it never showed up. It's real gold. It's from my mother, back when I was a kid. She was Catholic."

At this point the door opened quickly, admitting Detective Burnham. "Stop, Schouweiler! Hand that to me!" he shouted.

Tim looked at him, then at Elizabeth, then back at Burnham. As usual in his life, his options were few and he handed the cross and chain over to the detective.

"I couldn't help but hear what you two were saying," said Burnham. "So you found this in Hoffman's garden, Mrs. Elliot? Why didn't you give it to us?"

Elizabeth controlled her mounting anger and replied, "The reason I called you this morning, Mr. Burnham, was to report that I had visited Hoffman's backyard and found that icon in the mud of the rose garden. You didn't give me a chance to speak when I called but invited me to come down here, an invitation I accepted. If you were going to listen at the door you should have told Tim and me that, although I am sure that neither one of us has anything to hide. Our conduct here this afternoon would have been far different if Tim were guilty of anything wrong." She stopped for breath and wondered what legal issues might be involved in Burnham's taking the crucifix and listening to their talk. The cross, after all, was either her property, as its finder, or Tim's, as the original owner. Her words had certainly been intended for Tim's ears only, and she had had reason to think she was speaking to him in private. Elizabeth channeled her anger for a moment into thoughts about consulting with the ACLU. She remembered that in the 1960s the ACLU had used the Meetinghouse for some large gatherings. Surely someone in that group could help with this sort of question. But that, of course, would take time, and the preliminary hearing was going to run its course today whatever she might do right now.

"You will have to come with me, Mrs. Elliot, and make a statement about why you were there and exactly where you found this," answered Burnham.

He shouted at the door. Two uniformed officers came in through it; they must have been just outside the door waiting to be summoned. They took Tim by his arms and walked him out of the room. Tim made no resistance or protest as Elizabeth watched him go.

When Elizabeth returned home from the police station she sat down at her kitchen table almost stupefied. She did not notice the cat's shy greetings or see the birds out the window at her feeder. She thought of the rye dough in the refrigerator, but she was too paralyzed to consider resetting the loaves for the present. She felt helpless. Her efforts to help Tim had had terrible results. She was angry with the police, and with herself as well. Most of all, she felt confused. By the time she had finished making a statement to Burnham, he told her the preliminary hearing for Tim was just about to start. She had gone to East Cambridge to attended it in superior court. As she had feared, Tim was charged with murder. The judge, clearly influenced by Tim's homeless life, had set the bail at $250,000. Tim was led away quickly and Elizabeth did not even have an opportunity to catch his eye. As she sat in her kitchen, she wondered what a bail bondsman would charge for raising such bail. She would have to check into that. The situation seemed almost as overwhelming to Elizabeth as it clearly did to Tim. After a while, she began to cry bitterly.

Elizabeth was sure that Tim's obvious joy at seeing his cross again could not be connected with a fight and murder in John's rose garden. She feared, however, that she had put another piece of circumstantial evidence into the hands of the police. After she recovered from crying, Elizabeth's course was clear. She would help Tim fully establish his alibi or in some other way show that he was not guilty of this killing. She could not imagine who had really killed John Hoffman, but if he were not caught, another man would be held to account. Even the killer would be helped, Elizabeth hoped, when his identity was known to everyone, for only when sin is acknowledged can it be addressed. It is after a person has faced his transgressions that repentance can be hoped for.

But the responsibilities of a mother, an aunt, and a Quaker clerk do not stop just because of a resolution to help a jailed street person. Elizabeth recollected her appointment this evening with her niece Sarah and vowed to clear her mind of the police and of killings and be a good aunt. She stood up slowly, stretching her arthritic joints carefully and slowing shaking her head to clear her mind of Tim and the police. She turned on National Public Radio and noticed the cat for the first time, curled up on a kitchen chair. She stroked her cat and began to feel a little more normal.

She wiped the counter, turned on her oven, and began to make a batch of oatmeal raisin cookies. When she opened the refrigerator for milk and eggs, she saw the bread dough. She rescued it from its cold tomb, set the loaves, and put them on top of the stove. She was not sure how long they might require to rise again, since they had been thoroughly chilled. But she would be here for the rest of the day so timing no longer mattered to her.

She turned her attention once more to making cookies. She had the notion that all young people ate sweets and that oatmeal cookies must have nutritional value. Hence, she had a tendency to bake them for all occasions involving people under thirty.

Baking restored a sense of peace to her. It was a familiar task, and valued in women of her generation. As she worked in her kitchen, she began to feel some self-confidence returning and therefore could be a little more optimistic about the future. By the time all the cookies were out of the oven and Elizabeth was washing up from her efforts, the rye dough was returning to life. And when she had finished her supper, the loaves were ready to go into the oven. They came out brown and beautiful and filled the house with smells even better than cookies.

The bread was still warm but the cookies were cool and crisp when Sarah Curtis arrived at seven o'clock. She kissed her aunt at the front door and took off her coat, disentangling her long blond hair from the coat's zipper with some difficulty. She accepted tea and cookies with alacrity. Before Elizabeth could sit down, Sarah had gulped down one cookie and was reaching for another.

"It's so good of you to come by here," said Elizabeth. "At Meeting on Sundays there is always so much for me to do! I don't even have a chance to speak to my relatives!"

"Well, Aunt, I don't always come, but when I do it's nice to see you having care of the Meeting and doing the announcements. The clerkship seems to suit you."

"Oh, no," said Elizabeth, "I don't think so. Someone else should take over next year. I feel especially inadequate at Business Meetings. This past Sunday we even had a disruption caused by one of the homeless people, and if it hadn't been for Adam Chrisler, I certainly don't know what I would have done. I'm not fond of being Clerk."

"A disruption? That's unusual," observed Sarah. "You know, that same morning in Longfellow Park I saw the man who spoke in worship in a terrible argument with some-one."

Elizabeth started a bit but tried to ask calmly, and with-out undue concern, "Do you know who the other man was?"

"No," said Sarah. "I really didn't get a good look at him. I looked at the older man because he had spoken so hon-estly in Meeting for Worship." She had now downed an-other two cookies and asked for more tea.

"Did you happen to hear what they were discussing?" asked Elizabeth.

"No," said Sarah, laughing, "but anyway, is it really right to ask?"

"Of course not, not usually, but the man who spoke in worship may have been the focus of some truly unchristian thoughts at that time. I was just wondering what they might be. But tell me, how is school going?"

"It's good," answered Sarah. "The best thing is a women's studies class I'm taking. It's really changing my perceptions. We just read Virginia Woolf's *A Room of One's Own.* Have you read it?"

Elizabeth had to confess her ignorance. "I remember reading one of her short novels, but that's all. I'm afraid I probably missed the point of the story; I thought it was rather difficult."

"Well, Woolf herself isn't important. But the ideas about how limited our opportunities as women are in this society have been making more and more sense to me. When you look around Harvard, even though the women make up a lot of the best students, you don't see them going on to graduate school. Some don't even pursue professional work," added Sarah with a touch of astonishment in her voice. She reached for another cookie. "There's a big waste of women's talent, even in my generation," she concluded, shaking her head.

"What else are you taking this term?" asked Elizabeth.

"Organic chem and calculus and freshman physics," answered her niece. "It's all premed stuff. I'm done with all my biology requirements now, which is a relief."

Sarah leaned back in her chair and looked around the living room for a moment. "I want to ask the Clerk's advice about something. You see, I'm serious about my friend Steven, but I'm worried about our being so committed to different religions. Steve is Jewish, you know."

"I am all attention," said Elizabeth.

"I've known him since my freshman year. We've been going out together since last spring. The only real problem is the religion thing."

"Is Steven observant?"

"Oh, yes. He reads every Friday night at the Hillel services at Harvard. This fall I've been going to evening services with him. What I can understand about it, I like. Steve came to Quaker Meeting last Sunday, but just as an experiment.

"The thing is, if we were ever to get married and have kids, the kids wouldn't be Jewish, if I'm not a Jew. What counts is the mother, which is nice from a woman's perspective, but puts me in a bind."

"I see," answered Elizabeth. "On the other hand, if you and Steven were both Jewish and had children, the children would probably never become Quakers."

"You sound like my parents," said Sarah.

"It isn't as if the world has an oversupply of Quakers. We would be sad to lose you. But more seriously, all of this would be a minor concern to you if you truly felt led toward Jewish worship. That isn't what you seem to be saying. And to convert to anyone else's religion just for convenience or for children doesn't seem right to me."

"Oh, Aunt! You don't understand what love is like!"

Wounded, Elizabeth sat back in her chair. After forty years of a good marriage, she felt she had some claim to knowing what serious love was about. She looked as kindly as she could at Sarah and said, "You and Steven haven't invented love."

"Oh, I'm sorry! I'm always such a turkey! I come here to hear your advice and then I throw it in your face!"

"Don't worry"—Elizabeth laughed—"that's what almost everybody does with advice they don't want to hear. The important thing is for you to take your time about all of this. You and Steven are young, and neither of you has finished school. Wait and see where time takes you both. And where God leads you."

"Yes, I know we've got some time. But I'd like to move forward and get things resolved."

"Things will certainly be resolved; that won't be the problem. If you wait for God's time for a resolution there is a better chance everyone will be happy with the results. Happy, not just now, but in the long term, too."

Here Elizabeth was wise enough to stop. She asked Sarah to tell her more about Steven. This led to a lively conversation, at least on Sarah's side, covering Steven's family, his home, his friends at Harvard, and his many virtues. Elizabeth said she would like to meet him. Sarah and her aunt parted that evening promising each other to set a date for that purpose.

· · ·

Elizabeth had always wondered about the custom of reading the will of a deceased person to an assembled group.
Apart from the convenience of mystery writers, such gatherings seemed to have no usefulness. It seemed much more
businesslike to her to just send a copy of the will to everyone concerned. But perhaps the drama of reading a will
aloud appealed to others, if not to Elizabeth Elliot.

In any event, she was on her way to Bill Hoffman's house
the evening after Sarah had visited her for the reading of
John's will. She had been invited by Bill on the telephone
during the day to be a representative of Friends Meeting at
Cambridge, an institution that she guessed would likely
benefit from John's generosity one last time. She had
promised Hugo Coleman to call him tomorrow to let the
Finance Committee know what they could expect. Elizabeth was never worried about the Meeting's budget, confident that God's will would be done one way or another,
but those in charge of the finances felt differently about
God's concern for timely payments.

She arrived at Bill Hoffman's promptly at seven o'clock,
as instructed. Bill let her in with a thin smile and introduced her to one of the partners from his law firm, a man
named Bradford Smith. He chatted with Elizabeth while
several other people arrived. Mr. Bradford Smith was a
pompous man, loud and arrogant. He was wearing a large
college ring and a black tie with thin orange stripes, colors
that Elizabeth believed belonged to Princeton.

She and Bill were not the only persons from Quaker
Meeting present. Elizabeth saw Neil Stevenson come in,
and she smiled at him. Neil was a contemporary of hers
and a serious Quaker. Apparently he figured in the will
that was to be read. Erik Swensen was present, as Elizabeth
had expected. She was also introduced to a middle-aged

woman named Muriel Taylor who acted as a secretary and an accountant at the Swensen-Hoffman business. Bill then introduced her to an older man named Tom Hoffman, a distant relation of his, and to a woman named Anne White who had cleaned house for John twice each week for many years.

Bradford Smith beamed at them and asked them to sit down. When everyone had found a place he read the last will and testament of John Thomas Hoffman, dated seven years previously.

The will began with minor but gracious bequests to the company secretary and to John's house cleaner. Both women took the news with small smiles and remained silent. A gift of similar size was left to the American Friends Service Committee, a Quaker relief organization in Philadelphia. Erik Swensen was given a larger gift and John's best wishes for the future. He recommended the dissolution of their joint business but left it in Erik's hands to buy out John's share if that was what he wished.

Neil Stevenson of Friends Meeting was given John's rosebushes for grafting or transplantation. Neil shyly explained to the group that he shared John's hobby. Elizabeth herself had always loved roses, although she had no talent for growing them. For a moment, she wondered why she had not paid more attention to Neil, now a widower. Perhaps because he was so quiet, even by the standards of Quakers, it was possible to overlook him. As she sat in the crowded living room of Bill's apartment, Elizabeth couldn't help but have a moment's worth of daydreaming about inviting the good-looking Neil over to her house for tea. But she put the thought out of her mind and returned her attention to Mr. Smith's reading.

The will next indicated a gift of one hundred thousand

dollars to Friends Meeting at Cambridge without any re-
strictions on its use. Elizabeth was pleased and impressed
that John had not given his money for narrow purposes of
his own choosing; in her opinion that was an unnecessary
restriction of the working of the Spirit in the Meeting's
financial life. An equal amount was left to Swarthmore
College, John's alma mater, again without strings. The
remainder of his estate (which Mr. Bradford Smith added
was considerable) would go to his nephew and friend,
William Hoffman, who was also appointed as executor of
the will.

All in all, the will seemed much what an older and generous Friend might write. Dated seven years ago, it did not
seem to reflect any disquiet on John's part about his
wealth, the bulk of which was passing to his nephew. As a
lawyer, if not now as a judge, Bill Hoffman had been earn-
ing a great deal of money. This inheritance would complete his rise into the ranks of the very well-to-do. Elizabeth
wondered what John had meant on Sunday morning when
he had spoken of his will.

As the meeting broke up she had the opportunity to
speak to Bill as he handed her coat to her from the closet.

"It still has to be cleared with the Oversight Committee,
but Harriet and I have put down a memorial Meeting for
your uncle for a week from Saturday. How does that
sound?"

"Fine. That's fine."

As she put on her coat, Elizabeth said, "Could I borrow
a key to John's house? You have one, I suppose? I'll just
take a quick look to see if I can find anything like class
reunion lists or yearbooks that I could use to invite some
of his non-Quaker friends to the memorial Meeting." Bill
hesitated. "I'll need the key for only a day," she added.

Her request had clearly startled Bill Hoffman. There was a perceptible pause as he searched for a reply. It was, however, a reasonable request from an old and reliable Friend. Bill had, after all, asked her to be in charge of the memorial Meeting. Finally, he cleared his throat and said, "Certainly. The key's in the next room in my desk. I can get it for you in a moment. The police are done with the house now, so I am sure it's OK for you to go in. I'd go there myself and look through all his papers for you, but I'm under a lot of time pressure what with meeting with the Bar Association people about my appointment to the bench and going to the statehouse to appear before the Judiciary Committee. On top of that, I'm trying to clear up all the loose ends of my practice before I move to the bench and that entails more work than I first realized."

Elizabeth listened to this explanation politely and adjusted her hat as Bill fetched the key. She said good night and departed.

Because of the exchange about the key, Elizabeth left Bill's house a minute or two behind the others. On the street, however, she found Muriel Taylor vainly trying to start her car. The engine turned over repeatedly but would not catch. Elizabeth knocked on the car window from the passenger side and asked if there was anything she could do.

"I've been having lots of trouble with the electrical system of this car," said Muriel. "I guess the battery's finally died."

"We could go back to Bill's and call from there. If you'd rather deal with this in the morning, I'd be glad to give you a lift home."

"That's kind of you, but I live way out in Lexington," answered Muriel.

"Lexington is no problem. My car is just here across the street."

Muriel accepted with thanks and locked up her own car. Both women got into Elizabeth's '77 Chevrolet and began the trip out of Cambridge on Route 2.

"It was kind of John to remember me in his will," said Muriel. "I'm glad to say we always got on. I've been there fourteen years and I'll miss him."

"You'll stay on with the partnership, I suppose?" asked Elizabeth.

"No, I'm afraid not. Things have not been going too well with the business. Without John there, I'm afraid things will really fall apart."

"Oh?" said Elizabeth in her most encouraging tone. It was not like her to be nosy, but she felt the need to understand all that she could. What amazing and unattractive new skills she was developing, she thought as she changed lanes.

"Yes," said Muriel. "I hate to say it, but Erik has gotten himself and the business into real trouble. I'm sure that John was not even aware of the things that have happened recently. I do the books, you see, and I know how far Erik has taken us out on a limb. You know how soft the Boston real estate market is now. John Hoffman was always conservative in the risks he took. But lately he really wasn't paying attention to the work, and Erik's decisions aren't what you'd call conservative."

"I see," said Elizabeth. "I really don't understand much about business in general, but I've read in the newspapers that the real estate market is in a downturn."

"Downturn is a mild word for it," replied Muriel. She paused to give Elizabeth directions to her house. "Erik has been putting a lot of money into riskier projects. Many of his decisions were not even cleared with John. I'm sure things are falling apart now. Did you see the quarterly losses the Bank of Boston just posted? They're suffering from the real estate crash. If John had lived he would have found out at some point just how far Erik has extended partnership money. I'm sure they would have had a major falling-out. Anyway, I'm giving notice next week, and I'll be glad to be out of it. I'm afraid Erik may have been into very risky, even shady, transactions. That wasn't John's way and it isn't mine either."

"But the partnership had been a steady one through many years, hadn't it?" asked Elizabeth.

"That's true," responded Muriel, "but sometimes I can hardly recognize Erik lately. Things are messed up in his personal life. He's been through two divorces in five years, and one of his teenaged kids is in trouble with the law every other week. He's under a lot of stress."

"I see," responded Elizabeth, turning off the highway and stopping at the house Muriel indicated. The two women said good night.

Elizabeth turned her old Chevrolet around and began to retrace the road to Cambridge. Just as she got onto Route 2, however, the red light indicating a hot engine came on.

This is a bad night for women's cars, thought the tired Quaker with gentle exasperation. She slowed, but continued to drive east, hoping the light might go off of its own accord. It did not. Elizabeth remembered lectures from her husband on the subject of the red oil-pressure light on the dashboard. He had always impressed upon her that if that light ever came on, the car must be stopped immediately. But she could remember no conjugal instructions about the simple "hot" light.

In the late 1940s the Elliots' first car, purchased used,

had frequently boiled over. Because it was the first car Elizabeth had had any close acquaintance with, she had accepted such behavior as normal. The Elliots had carried a couple of gas cans filled with water in the trunk. She had many memories of being beside highways in New Hampshire with Michael, the engine spitting water and steam. Thus, when the Chevrolet boiled over just as she reached the township of Arlington, Elizabeth knew what was happening. She pulled off Route 2 and onto a residential street, then shut off the engine. The car stopped, but noises from under the hood continued as the radiator vented itself of its frustrations.

Elizabeth could see no reason to open the hood and inspect the engine. She had no water, and it was late. She wanted to go home and deal with the problem in the morning. She knocked at the front door of the house nearest where the car had come to rest. An elderly man cautiously opened the door, but then swung it fully open when he saw Elizabeth. He spoke with a strong accent, making short replies as she explained the situation and asked if she might use the telephone. The man invited her in with a wide sweep of his hand.

"My name is Demos. The phone is here. Call anywhere!"

Elizabeth thanked Mr. Demos and called her younger son. After five rings she realized he was not at home. She felt some maternal concern about where he might be at night, but she quickly concluded it was not her business. She hesitated to call her pediatrician son. Between the demanding hours of his job and the needs of his own small child, she was sure that providing a ride for his mother in Arlington would not be a welcome task. On an impulse, she picked up the telephone book next to the telephone and looked up Neil Stevenson's number.

He answered promptly. Elizabeth apologized profusely, explained her predicament, and asked if he could give her a ride to Cambridge.

"Of course!" said Neil quickly and without a hint of dismay at having to leave his house. "Tell me where you are."

Elizabeth explained where she had left Route 2 and put Mr. Demos on the line to explain exactly where she was. Judging from the part of the conversation she overheard, Neil had some difficulties in understanding the Greek's directions, but in the end Mr. Demos seemed pleased. "Good-bye!" he said triumphantly into the receiver, and beamed at Elizabeth. "He will be here soon. From Cambridge, it's quick."

Elizabeth declined a drink but accepted the easy chair she was offered. On a coffee table beside the chair were several photographs. Inquiring about them led to a conversation, lively on Mr. Demos's side, about his children and grandchildren. After the last descendant had been named and minutely described, the doorbell rang. It was Neil.

Thanking Mr. Demos warmly for his help and promising to have the car removed from his curb soon, Elizabeth departed. Neil, apparently a gentleman of the old school, held open the passenger door of his car for her. Elizabeth was sure such behavior would not be acceptable to the younger women of Meeting, and she felt ambivalent about accepting it. But since Neil had driven into the darkness of outer Arlington to rescue her, she put any reproof out of her mind.

Both Quakers were in the mood to talk as Neil drove to Cambridge. He inquired after the symptoms of Elizabeth's car and pronounced the water pump a likely culprit.

"On a seventy-seven car, American-made no less, the water pump can go out anytime. I'm glad you were nearby and that it wasn't any later in the evening. Have you thought about buying a newer car, just for the safety factor?"

Ambivalence again filled Elizabeth, who was not sure if she should be flattered by Neil's evident concern or annoyed by the implications of patronization.

"I've been thinking about a newer car, actually, but I'm still only at the thinking stage. I hate to give up on things that can be fixed. What would Woolman think!"

To change the subject she quickly asked, "What did you make of the will we heard earlier this evening, Neil? It didn't reflect the changing values John mentioned in worship just before his death."

"No. It was a standard will, I suppose. Whatever John was trying to express that First-day didn't seem to be standard stuff. I suppose he didn't have time to write a new will."

"So it seems. Did you know John well?"

"No, I didn't."

"None of us did. Except perhaps Bill. I wished John had lived much longer. I think he and Meeting would both have been well served by a deeper acquaintance."

"That could well be," said Neil, slowing the car. He dropped Elizabeth off in front of her house on Concord Avenue. She thanked him and asked if he would be interested in coming to her house someday for Sunday dinner. Neil indicated he would welcome the idea and the pair parted.

The following morning Elizabeth called her son the engineer while he was at breakfast. She explained what had happened to her car and asked for his help in getting it to a garage for repair. Without enthusiasm, he agreed to take care of it, saying additionally that she must consider buying a newer vehicle. Elizabeth expressed her thanks for his help and ignored his well-meant advice. Her mind was elsewhere.

Elizabeth tidied up her kitchen and put on her navy-blue coat and walking shoes. The weather had cleared again, and she was glad to fill the bird feeders and then walk to John Hoffman's house on Royal Avenue. She let herself in, putting her coat in the front closet, just as she used to do when visiting John with other Friends for Quaker committee meetings. She paused for a moment to remember all the Quaker work which had been accomplished by committees in John's living room. His had been an active life of service to what he saw as God's work.

She sat down at John's desk and began a careful search for anything that might pertain to a new will or John's financial ideas of late. She comforted herself with the thought that she would also keep her eyes open for anything that would help her to locate John's old school friends so they could be invited to the memorial.

A man of John Hoffman's age accumulates many papers, and he did not keep anything in order. Happily for Elizabeth, all of his business papers were kept at work. Here at home he had numerous records about his own finances, about Quaker committee work (dating back to the 1950s), and about roses. It took a long time for Elizabeth to examine all the papers and satisfy herself that there was no new will kept in his desk. She did, however, find two booklets from class reunions at Swarthmore and the yearbook from John's graduating class. She was interested to see he had been very active in sports in his college days.

Both reunion booklets contained addresses of class members, and since Swarthmore College had been very small when John had been enrolled (and the numerous intervening years had no doubt thinned his class roll) Elizabeth saw that she could easily write to everyone in John's class and inform them of his death and the memorial Meeting. It eased her conscience to have found what she was supposed to be here for. She did not, however, end her search.

She checked the kitchen table and the bedroom nightstand and dresser for papers or notes. She found nothing. She wondered if John kept a journal. Such a document might well record his intentions about changing his finances and his will. Many serious Quakers were in the habit of keeping journals: they were meant to record not just day-to-day events but the growth of the author in the life of the Spirit. Elizabeth herself kept a journal, although she did not devote as much time to it as she had meant to when she was young and had her first one. The Cambridge Friends Meeting sometimes held meetings of interested persons on the subject of journal writing. A thoughtful and serious Quaker like John Hoffman would be the sort of Friend to keep a journal. She asked herself where she would keep a journal if she lived in this house.

Elizabeth sat down in the living room to think. Something seemed strange to her. She could not put her finger on it. She needed to let her mind rest and approach the problem in its own way. After a time she decided there would be no harm done if she used John's kitchen to make herself a cup of tea. She immediately set about the familiar task. Soon she was seated at the kitchen table with some English breakfast tea.

As she sipped the tea it struck her: she had not seen a single Bible at John's desk, in his living room, or in his bedroom. Confident that John Hoffman would own several Bibles, volumes on Quaker history, and perhaps some devotional books, she stood up and went in search of them.

Elizabeth discovered that a small hallway led from the living room to the back door of the house and to a door that went down to the cellar. One side of this hallway was lined with bookshelves where John had arranged his small library. The top shelf held half a dozen Bibles in various translations and two concordances. The next shelf contained a mixture of Quaker history and publications by and about the American Friends Service Committee. The last shelf contained a long row of slender green volumes. Elizabeth opened the first and found a number of pages describing rosebush performances and problems for the year 1963. She almost returned the volume to the shelf, but on a whim leafed forward in the volume another dozen pages more. On page 20, the volume began a record of John's activities day by day, and his thoughts, in the manner of a Quaker journal. The next volume covered 1964; again it was misleading at the beginning, appearing to be only a gardener's record. But after twenty or so pages concerning roses, the volume became a carefully recorded journal. The police, thought Elizabeth, must have looked only at the first dozen pages of these volumes and put them back as unhelpful. The green books ran along the bottom shelf, covering time up through the present year. She opened the most recent volume just to be sure it was complete through last week. It was: John had recorded his thoughts and actions through last Sunday. Elizabeth felt real apprehension for Bill and for the Meeting community as she looked down at the pages of the journal. After a moment's consideration, and with a glance at her watch, Elizabeth decided to take the journal home with her. It wasn't like her to postpone a moment of truth, but she suddenly felt old and apprehensive about what she might find. She cleared up her tea things and got her coat from the closet. Carefully locking the door, she went out onto the front step and buttoned up her coat.

The walk home was unpleasant, for she felt oppressed. She had had no idea that the responsibilities of Clerk would involve her in reading another person's journals and lying, or nearly lying, to such good Quakers as Bill Hoffman. She wondered for a moment if she were exceeding her responsibilities as Clerk. Things had been much more simple when she was at home raising children and letting her husband deal with the difficulties of Meeting business. Another reason for Elizabeth's depression, however, was that she was afraid of what John's journal might tell her. She scolded herself for her lack of faith as she walked, but once home, she had a good lunch and a hot bath before she began to read.

6

On hearing this Jesus said, "There is still one thing lacking: sell everything you have and distribute to the poor, and you will have riches in heaven; and come, follow me." At these words his heart sank; for he was a very rich man. When Jesus saw it he said, "How hard it is for the wealthy to enter the kingdom of God! It is easier for a camel to go through the eye of a needle than for a rich man to enter the kingdom of God."

Luke 18: 22–25

Elizabeth sat at her kitchen table with the journal. With pleasure, she noted that John Hoffman had written in a neat hand and had recorded his entries clearly. After the gardening pages, the journal began with New Year's Day of the present year and gave details of John's activities every day. She skimmed the entries of the winter and spring, but began to read each entry starting July 1.

There was little about John's business dealings. She thought she should look at earlier years to see if this had been the case in the past. Throughout the journal, Quaker business matters and information about John's extended family were recorded meticulously. Birthdays, and presents sent, were recorded even in the case of cousins and other more distant relatives. She had not known John was so devoted to people distantly related to him. Perhaps, she mused, this was not unusual for a single and childless man, now grown old.

Bill Hoffman had received a generous birthday gift of money from his uncle this past July. Elizabeth wondered if this generosity was an annual event. Since John had known Bill as a child she supposed the pattern of a substantial monetary gift may have been established years ago, perhaps to help him and his middle-class parents set aside something for college tuition. Such gifts can be difficult to end, especially when the giver is prosperous.

The journal also detailed many events of the Cambridge Friends Meeting. Conversations with people were briefly summarized. Most concerned Finance Committee and Building Committee questions. To Elizabeth's surprise, a number of conversations about liberation theology were mentioned, apparently in exchanges with Adam Chrisler. Liberation theology, the radical religious perspective developed in Central America in response to the desperate needs of the poor and dispossessed, was not something in which Elizabeth would expect John to be interested. She couldn't understand the circumstances in which these conversations took place. The two men certainly seemed an unlikely pair. In an entry in mid-September, John had noted "Feel sorrow, but must speak against same-sex marriage question at next Business Meeting." This, of course, he had done on the Sunday just past. As far as Elizabeth could recall, the sorrow had not been evident, but she did not doubt that it had been there. She had often noted that sorrow and self-righteousness were threads that Quakers found easy to weave together.

The arthritis in Elizabeth's hands forced her to stop reading for a moment and lay the journal down flat on the kitchen table. Sometimes her hands were nearly pain free, but now and then they made her wince. Rubbing her hands gently together, she leaned forward and continued to peruse the pages of John's neat hand.

Several entries on personal spiritual matters were quite long. John had copied out extensive portions of George Fox's writings. There were scraps of wisdom from various mystics, Quaker and non-Quaker. John wrote briefly about his own experiences in prayer, but he wrote with feeling. Elizabeth respected the effort he had put into spiritual living. Again, she found herself resolving to spend more time on her own journal. Especially now that she was Clerk, it seemed necessary to live as clearly and as deeply as she could.

Elizabeth turned to the pages which described John's last weekend alive. Saturday's entry had notes under a heading called "New Will! And Divestment Proceedings: take to Bill." The list read:

To be divided up before the end of this calendar year:

AFSC	$1,500,000
American University, El Salvador	$500,000
The Catholic Worker: New York, Philadelphia and Boston Houses:	$500,000 *each*
Christ Church Soup Kitchen, Cambridge	99% *of residue*
Cambridge Meeting	1% *of residue*

Beneath the list was a note: "How to implement this now: and then what to live on? Let Bill handle liquidation and disbursement."

Elizabeth Elliot took a deep breath to consider what an unusual retirement plan she was reading. She knew just enough legal language to understand that the term "residue" meant all that was left over; this meant that John Hoffman intended, before the end of the year, to give all of his wealth away. That certainly made the query "then what to live on?" an appropriate one. In any event, the journal entry bore no relation to what had been read at Bill Hoffman's apartment the previous evening.

Elizabeth looked at the list of organizations. The AFSC reference she understood well: it stood for the American Friends Service Committee, the Quaker relief organization to which most Quakers contributed some money. The AFSC had won the Nobel Peace Prize after World War II. Respectable and law-abiding, it was the kind of organization to which a wealthy Quaker businessman might be expected to leave some money. But so much?

The next entry in John's list, however, was quite different in character.

American University in El Salvador was, if Elizabeth remembered correctly, the university at which six Jesuit priests had been killed by government thugs the previous year. The priests had been active in writing about and working for "liberation theology." They had labored for the church, but as they had understood it, the church belonged to the poor. This radical perspective had made them enemies of the government. Elizabeth had not known that John had any interest in Central America, nor that people associated so clearly with the liberation theology movement would ever figure in his will. Either the gift revealed a side of John Hoffman she had never seen or it showed he had been undergoing a significant change in values late in life.

The next entry was also radically different from what one might expect from John. The Catholic Worker organization, dating back to the 1930s, was a group of soup kitchens organized around political ideas. In addition to a commitment to pacifism, which Elizabeth and all Quakers could respect, the Catholic Workers followed a political line somewhere between socialism and anarchism. She respected the organization because of its ceaseless efforts to feed the very poor, but she would not have expected John to give a staggering amount of money to a radical group, however much it might quote the gospel.

The Christ Church gift was more understandable. The ecumenical soup kitchen had existed at Christ Church, in the middle of Harvard Square, for some years now. It was a good program, and the Quaker Meeting supported it with money and with volunteers, usually students. Still, 99 percent of the residue of a millionaire's estate was a great deal to be given to one soup kitchen. Elizabeth wondered what the annual budget of a soup kitchen was, and she wondered how such a large gift might be used.

The gift to Friends Meeting at Cambridge was no surprise, of course, but when seen next to John's generous gifts to soup kitchens, even Catholic ones, the gift to the Meeting seemed small. In fact, as Clerk, it was a little difficult not to feel a bit hurt by John's notation of 1 percent of residue. But when Elizabeth reflected upon the different needs of wealthy Quaker Meetings, on the one hand, and of soup kitchens, on the other, she could appreciate why John might have viewed his gifts as equitable. The plan as a whole was as unlike the old John Hoffman as one could imagine. Elizabeth wondered where, or from whom, John had been receiving such a different vision of life. Was this apparent change one of growth and a new selflessness, or was it only an old man's desperation to find meaning for life in old age?

Elizabeth contributed money, but not her time, to the local soup kitchen effort. She often felt she should be doing more. And she knew she should be following her government's actions in Central America more closely than she did. But again, she wondered how John had become sensitized both to the problems of the homeless in the Cambridge area and to the situation in El Salvador. Perhaps it was all the mysterious process of God's will being played out in the life of a faithful and prayerful Quaker. But Elizabeth wondered if some members of the Meeting might feel John must have been under undue influence from someone. It certainly was a mystery how this process had begun in John and who, if anyone, had been nurturing it. Elizabeth's mind turned to the John Woolman she had been reading earlier in the week. It was easy for Quaker saints like Woolman and George Fox to "simplify" their lives to the point of poverty, but could the respectable John Hoffman really have traveled down the path trod in early times by the greatest of Quakers?

In rereading the entry Elizabeth noted the words "take

to Bill.'' She wondered if these ideas and this list had been
taken to Bill Hoffman on Sunday, when uncle and nephew
must have seen each other in Meeting. The implication of
immediate action would explain the note questioning what
John would live on now. It was not easy to see what he
would have lived on if he had given all of his wealth away.
Could John have expected help from his nephew even if he
had voluntarily made himself destitute?

Elizabeth turned to the entry for Sunday. It contained a
note saying ''Spoke in Worship about financial changes.
Feel led in my efforts to change and feel progress is now
rapid. Great joy, day and night! Many years have been
wasted but perhaps all this was necessary for me to see and
understand. Spoke in Business Meeting against homosexual marriage. Felt led in my speech although still sorrow-
ful. Adam Chrisler to come here tomorrow afternoon to
speak to me about marriage question.

''Much work to do tomorrow in the garden: will be off
work because of Columbus Day. What to do about the
partnership after New Year's?''

Elizabeth looked at the page that should have contained
an entry for Monday, the day of John's death. It was blank,
as were the pages following. The journal had ended with
Sunday's events. Probably John was in the habit of recording his entries in the evening. Monday evening he had
been lying dead in his garden. Someone else had written a
final entry, but not on journal paper.

Sitting in her kitchen, holding the dead man's writings
in her hand, Elizabeth felt true anger. John Hoffman had
been a good and thoughtful man. He had been undergoing real spiritual change, yet he had been struck down
and killed by someone who now denied the killing. Forti-
fied by her anger, she considered all she knew about the

murder and all she had read. She carefully copied out the entries in the journal for the last two days. Pausing at the kitchen sink to take a dose of blood pressure medicine, she got her coat and walked back to the Hoffman house on Royal Avenue and returned the journal to its place. The police could look for it if they wished, but for the present Elizabeth was not going to volunteer any more information to the Cambridge police department. She now distrusted Burnham too much to deal with him voluntarily.

As she left John's house, locking the front door after her, Elizabeth could not help but think that it might still contain something else the police had missed. She had certainly not searched the place carefully. Adam Chrisler had been expected by John on Monday. She wondered if she might be able to find evidence that he had come. Papers of some sort detailing the startling financial changes which John was considering might still be in his house. Or would he have given them all to his lawyer and nephew? Elizabeth was reluctant to return the only house key to Bill. After some indecision, she walked to Harvard Square and had a copy of the house key made at Dickson's hardware store. As she waited for the clerk to do the job, she promised herself not to use the key unless it seemed absolutely necessary. She recognized such bargaining with herself as compromising with the devil, but she put that thought out of her mind. Remembering that Tim Schouweiler was in police custody and had no one to speak up for him, she was angry with the murderer. Her thoughts were rationalizations, but they allowed her to stand quietly as she listened to the rasping of the locksmith's key replicator.

Leaving Harvard Square, Elizabeth walked home by way of Bill Hoffman's apartment. She left his copy of John's key in the mailbox. After she returned home, she realized how tired she was, but she forced herself to address the details of organizing the memorial for John. She wrote to his Swarthmore classmates. Then she sat down in her kitchen and called several of the older members of Meeting to inform them of the date and time of the memorial service and asked each to call several other people she named. This covered the older set of the Quaker community. Next Elizabeth called two of the younger Quakers, asking them to spread the word. Biting her lip, she then dialed Hugo Coleman's number. She left a message on his answering machine with the information about the memorial, asking him to call back. She felt uncomfortable about talking to Hugo now that she knew that John's plans about giving to the Meeting were so much up in the air at the time of his death. She knew, too, that she must talk to Bill Hoffman about what the journal contained. This was a task that she dreaded but could see no way, in conscience, to escape. Compromising with herself, she called Bill at home, hoping he would be at work. She reached only his answering machine and left a message thanking him for the use of the key to John's house and asking him to return her call.

Finally, with a sigh produced by so much telephoning, Elizabeth called Adam Chrisler. He was at home and answered promptly, still sounding hoarse but more recognizable.

"I'm sorry to interrupt; I assume you are writing," began Elizabeth. "We've scheduled the memorial Meeting for John and due to the short notice, I'm calling a number of people to let them know."

"Right. I was at the Meetinghouse this morning and saw the sign Harriet had posted."

"Good." She changed her tone of voice and continued

in a businesslike way. "I received a phone call from Detective Burnham of the Cambridge police and I was wondering if you had, too."

"Yes, I did," said Adam, "He had learned that John and I often disagreed about Meeting business and he wanted to know where I was on Monday afternoon. I told him I was in Boston, at city hall, in the Bread-Not-Bombs protest. I was with Chris Richardson of the Meeting, and she can vouch for me until about five P.M. when I left. The Red Line had shut down for some reason. Park Street station was a zoo."

"I see," said Elizabeth. She wondered what she might say without revealing she had been reading a dead man's private journal. Although she felt bad about lying to anyone, she continued. "I had wondered if you saw John sometime on Monday; he happened to mention to me that you were going to speak to him about the same-sex marriage question. I thought you were going to stop by and see him."

There was a pause. "Well, yes, I did intend to take the train to Harvard Square and walk to his house to talk. That was why I left the protest at five. But the subway wasn't running at all, and you know how bad the buses are, even on a regular day, much less a holiday. I waited for a bus at Park Street for a while but none came by. So I gave up and went to the Meetinghouse on Beacon Hill. I had supper there with a number of people from the demonstration. I tried calling John, to explain why I wasn't coming. There was no answer. I spoke with Jean Nyman there at Beacon Hill. I told the police they could check with her and she could say where I was between five and six. It was close to seven when we all finished with supper. She and I ate together and discussed the need for us to do something more organized and visible to oppose the military buildup in the Gulf. After supper I took a bus back to Cambridge.

"Who can say how things might have been if I had been able to go to John's," concluded Adam. "But I have to go, Elizabeth. I have a lot of work to catch up on here." He sounded quite tense, and Elizabeth realized this was not a good time to ask further questions. She had, of course, no authority to ask anyone anything except in her capacity as Clerk, and Clerks lead only by persuasion. She wished Adam a good day.

Elizabeth considered whether an argument over Meeting business could lead to murder. She did not think that Quakers were saints. Nor were pacifists never violent. She felt sure that if a Meeting member were involved, however, he or she would eventually break down from the stress of guilt. The truth would be told. She wondered if the murder could have been premeditated, or if, as seemed more likely, the action had been an impulse and was now deeply regretted.

Elizabeth's thinking was interrupted by the telephone. Hugo Coleman was returning her call. John Hoffman's gift of $100,000 to the Meeting, indicated in his will, was good news to the Finance Committee. The money was especially welcome since there were to be no restrictions on its use. Hugo said the money should go straight into the general fund, and the budget for this year could be met with money left over for the building fund. Elizabeth responded that a Business Meeting would have to consider such an important decision, and after a tense moment or two, Hugo agreed.

Even if the will that had been read was the only legally valid document, Elizabeth wanted to satisfy herself better about what John was thinking shortly before he died. As part of a memorial to him, the Meeting should see that his final struggles and changes were respected and act accordingly. Apart from all that, she wondered if the Meeting should accept money that was coming its way as the result of violence. She did not, however, raise this idea with Hugo. If other people had similar thoughts, it would come up at Business Meeting. Elizabeth and Hugo briefly discussed the coming memorial and then said good-bye.

She sat down at the kitchen table and idly looked at the newspaper. By chance she skimmed the Science section, not her usual habit, and there she found an article about arthritis and some of the new theories about how it develops and how it might be treated in the future. Fully absorbed by something which described her own pains so well, Elizabeth did not see the cat, or even know Sparkle was in the room, until she rubbed up against her mistress's legs. Not wanting her nylons covered with cat hair, Elizabeth reached down and stroked the cat until she jumped up on the kitchen chair.

"Listen to this, Friend," said Elizabeth to the cat. She read the part of the article which said doctors hoped to be able to treat the cause, rather than the symptoms, of arthritis in the future. "It's all internal chemistry, you see, that brings about the inflammation. Sometimes even in children! What a curse that must be!"

Sparkle began to purr. Elizabeth returned her whole attention to the paper. A man had been found stabbed on one of MIT's sidewalks the previous evening. He was alive but unconscious at Cambridge City Hospital.

I wonder if Detective Burnham is ever involved in cases where the victim doesn't die, thought Elizabeth. It's quite arbitrary to only investigate killings. But perhaps this man will recover and be able to name the attacker.

Elizabeth gathered up the paper and put it on the recycling stack. Looking at the towering pile of loose news-print, she sighed, got out her full supply of grocery bags, and began to put the newspapers into bags in a neater fashion. A reliable car, she realized, would be helpful when it came to trips to the recycling center. But taking things to a recycling depot in a new car would surely be a kind of hypocrisy. She turned on National Public Radio to keep her company and labored on with the job.

The ringing telephone sent Sparkle running for the basement. It was Bill Hoffman.

"Were you able to find anything from Swarthmore that could help you locate Uncle John's friends from school days?" asked Bill.

"Yes, I've a good class list and I've written to the people listed in his most recent reunion booklet," answered Elizabeth. "I also found one of his yearbooks. I didn't know John was so athletic."

"Yes," said Bill, "he still rowed three times a week on the Charles from May to October. He was in great shape." He added in a strained voice, "I guess your search through Uncle John's house didn't turn up anything else of interest?"

"No, not much," replied Elizabeth uncomfortably. "But I've been remembering a comment that John made to me last week as well as what he said at Meeting on Sunday morning, and I'm sure that he must have intended very substantial changes in his financial life. Didn't he mention anything to you about that?"

"Only in a vague way, just after Meeting for Worship. My uncle had some rather surprising thoughts now and then. People in our family can be a bit manic, but it doesn't go deep. Uncle John was a conservative Quaker and a deeply conservative businessman. His weekend reexamination of his life wouldn't have led to any real changes. Not after the dust had settled."

"So he didn't give you any specific instructions for a new will? Or tell you that he wanted to divide up his estate even before he died?"

Bill paused and then replied, "No, Friend, he did not." There was finality in his voice.

Elizabeth, quieting her conscience as best she could, took a deep breath and said, "Bill, I'm sorry, but I don't think that can all be true. On Sunday John mentioned to me that he meant to speak to you and give you what I understood were specific instructions about dividing up his wealth. 'Divestment,' I think he called it. Didn't he find you at Meeting on Sunday?"

"We did speak briefly, Elizabeth, and he did talk about what you mention, but only in the vaguest way. It was a sort of temporary storm. What would he have lived on if he had given his money away? Uncle John was not irresponsible. Think of the life he led! His interest in 'divestment' was unclear and undefined and wouldn't have lasted."

Elizabeth let this answer stand. She changed her tone and asked matter-of-factly, "Detective Burnham has been asking some people where they were on Monday after-noon. Have you been asked that, too?"

"Yes, and if I had wanted to establish a clear alibi I certainly could have done a better job of it. It was Colum-bus Day, so my secretary had the day off. I was at work, of course, lawyers always end up working Monday holidays, but the staff gets the day off. I worked from early morning until four, and then, since it was a holiday, I went to Cen-tral Square, to a place called The Station, and had a drink there with Tom Redburn from Meeting."

Elizabeth was a bit disoriented, as she often was when

talking to the younger members of Meeting. The Station was a gay bar, and Tom Redburn was one of the most openly gay Quakers in New England. In Elizabeth's day, simply stopping at a bar and drinking alcohol would have been unthinkable. She knew that many Quakers did now drink, but it was a fact she found difficult to accept.

"I see. Well, I'm glad that Tom will be able to vouch for your whereabouts."

"At least for a little while he can, but I didn't stay at The Station long. I caught a bus up to Harvard Square because the Red Line didn't seem to be running, and I walked home. I read for a couple of hours, catching up on my *Car and Driver* and *Sports Illustrated* subscriptions. Then I went for a quick supper at the Greenhouse Café in Harvard Square. I eat there a lot and the help knows me. But you see, from a police perspective, I could have gone over to Royal Avenue from my apartment and beaten my uncle to death before going to the Square. No one at the Greenhouse will be sure of the exact time I came in. Even I don't know precisely when I arrived and left."

"These things are difficult," sighed Elizabeth.

"But it's up to the police to prove that I, or anyone else, did something wrong," responded Bill. His tone changed abruptly as he said, "I should go back to work now."

Elizabeth said good-bye. She sat down to consider all she had learned and to seek guidance for her next step.

Saturday dawned cold but clear. It was a fine October day. Elizabeth had spent a bad night and welcomed the dawn. She had tossed and turned from midnight onwards, thinking about Tim. People like Tim always started at a disadvantage, and they did not get a second chance once something in their lives had gone wrong. On the streets they were seen as victims by some and lost causes by others, and dismissed by nearly everyone. Elizabeth knew Tim well enough to know he had talents. Unfortunately, from what she had seen of Tim since he was picked up by the police, he was losing his capacity to react to events. Elizabeth feared he might even agree to sign things which were not true. Tim was alone and in pain; his normal state of living was one of emotional confusion, and she feared things could go very badly for him in jail. As she ate her breakfast the Clerk continued down this train of thought. Abruptly, she decided she must snap her mind out of this spiral and take some action.

Elizabeth put on her coat and hat and walked to Harvard Square, where she caught the Red Line to Central Square. As she came out of the underground, she asked a couple of the homeless men sitting on the subway stairs if they could tell her where to find the Salvation Army building. Both men were shabbily dressed and both were dirty. One of the men was smoking a cigarette. He continued to smoke and ignored both Elizabeth and her question. The other man, however, looked up at her and said in a heavy South Boston accent: "Yeah, I know the Sally. About three blocks from here. How about I show you where it is and you give me a buck for my trouble?"

Elizabeth agreed, and the two walked down Massachusetts Avenue, almost to the edge of the MIT campus. The wind was picking up and the temperature seemed to be dropping. She felt chilled through her coat. The man she was with stopped walking and stood mutely on the sidewalk. A low building stood on the right side of the avenue and Elizabeth's guide nodded to it. He accepted a dollar and walked back up toward Central Square.

An old and apparently homeless woman was sitting on

the sidewalk in front of the Salvation Army building, leaning against the building's wall near the front doors. Elizabeth walked to the doors, nodding slightly at the woman who was looking directly in her face. She tried to open the front door, but it was locked. She paused, uncertain as to what to do next. The woman on the sidewalk, still studying Elizabeth, said, "They lock up between things here and lunch ain't here yet, sweetie. But if you knock real loud you might be able to get their attention. You ain't looking for a meal, I'll bet."

"No. I'm looking for someone who works here." Saying this, Elizabeth knocked as loudly as she could on one of the doors.

"Lots of people work here, seems like," answered the woman on the sidewalk. "There's big business in doing good in this town. Are you thinking of volunteering? If you are, let me tell you to forget it. We hate you, see? You're better off wherever you're from."

While Elizabeth was considering how she might answer, the door of the building opened and a middle-aged man stuck his head out.

"Hello, my name is Elizabeth Elliot. I'm from the Quaker Meeting up near Harvard Square. I'm looking for two men who worked here last Monday."

"You might come in out of the cold," said the man, motioning her indoors. "Why are you looking for some of our people?"

The door shut behind Elizabeth and closed out the wind. "I know it sounds strange, but it's important for me to be sure where a friend of mine was last Monday afternoon. A man in our Meeting was murdered, I'm afraid, and the police have picked up a homeless man who often comes to our Meetings on Sunday."

"Who's that?" asked the Salvation Army officer.

"A fellow named Tim, Tim Schouweiler."

"Oh, the big guy with scraggly hair? Yes, we know Tim, although I didn't know his last name."

"Nor did we, actually, but the police tell me that it's Schouweiler. The police are focusing their interest on Tim, and it seems to me that Tim is pretty overwhelmed by the situation. He tells me that he was here for lunch on that day and stayed after lunch to get a shower. Someone left him alone in the room where you keep the clothes, and he says he curled up there and slept away the afternoon."

"That last part sounds familiar," answered the man. "Come back into the kitchen and let's talk with Carl Over-dahl. I think he's the man you want."

Carl Overdahl turned out to be a large and friendly man who said he was pleased to meet a Quaker, he knew Tim well, he certainly remembered the events of that Monday, and all that Tim had said to Elizabeth was true.

"It was my fault. I left him alone in the clothing room when I got called away for a while. Then I forgot to check to see that he had really gone. Just a bit before six I went back to that room to turn out the lights before going home. Tim was dead asleep on top of a couple of coats. I had to shake him to get him awake. It took quite a bit of time to get him up and out of there."

"Could he have come and gone sometime during the afternoon without your knowing?" asked Elizabeth.

"No. We keep things locked up around here, and if he'd left each door he went through would've locked after him. He would've had to pound on the door to get inside, and we wouldn't let Tim in during hours when we're not open. No, I'm sure he was there all afternoon."

Elizabeth thanked Carl for his time and asked him to call

Detective Burnham and report what he knew. Carl said he'd be glad to do so.

"And thank you, Mrs. Elliot, for coming down here to tell us. We had wondered a bit about Tim. He usually comes every day for lunch, but he's been gone quite a while now, hasn't he?"

Elizabeth again thanked Carl for his helpfulness. She left the Salvation Army building the way she had come in. The front door locked behind her as she found out by testing it once she was outside on the street. The older woman who had been sitting on the sidewalk was no longer there. Elizabeth hoped she had gone somewhere to get out of the cold wind that was now blowing more seriously than ever.

After retracing her steps to Central Square and catching the outbound Red Line, Elizabeth emerged from the underground at Harvard Square. She crossed the common quickly, ignoring, as best she could, the homeless gathered there. Her energies for contemplating the life of the destitute had been used up for the day. She walked up Concord Avenue, grateful that the wind was now at her back. Her fingers were stiff from cold as well as arthritis when she reached her house, but she opened her mailbox with her palms and took out Saturday's mail. When she shut her front door behind her, she sighed with relief. The house was warm and quiet, and Sparkle greeted her with unusual friendliness.

A cup of Earl Grey at the kitchen table and a few minutes watching the juncos at her feeder revived Elizabeth's spirits. She looked through her mail. In addition to the usual bills and catalogs, there was a personal letter from her sister-in-law Pearl. With pleasure Elizabeth opened the envelope and took out the letter.

Dear Elizabeth,

It was so good to see you last Fourth of July. I do hope you can come down again and see us. I've been meaning to write since July, but with one thing and another the time has just flown by. I hope autumn is beautiful now, as it should be in New England. Have you been on a color tour? When I think of your yard, I hope you can hire help for your raking, or have one of your boys come over. Don't work on it yourself! Joints our age must be treated kindly.

Sarah calls us regularly and sometimes writes. We gather she is serious about this Steven of hers. We knew, when she went off to Harvard, it was unlikely she'd go out with Quaker boys. That was the reason, you may recall, I wanted her to go to Swarthmore or Earlham. I must admit, I was quite apprehensive about Harvard as a whole for her, but of course knowing you were nearby was a help to me.

I thought that the worst that might come from her Harvard years would be an Episcopalian or Lutheran son-in-law. Or more likely, a nonreligious one. I never even thought about Catholics or Jews. I guess I was being awfully parochial!

But now what's a mother to do? I know our kids must choose their own paths. Still, I worry. What if Sarah marries Steven and they have children? How would they be raised? I've tried to ask Sarah to think about such things, but she gets angry with me. She thinks I'm encroaching.

Have you met Steven? I'd be glad to know your opinion of him. Jim and I fear Sarah may not come home at Christmas. She says she's invited to Steven's

house to meet his relatives. We are considering inviting them both here for New Year's. Steven is a senior
this year. I'm not sure where he will be next year and
I'm afraid it could be anywhere, in which case Sarah
might not come home next Christmas either.

Does Sarah talk to you about any of this? She men-
tions to us that she sees you sometimes and that's why
I ask. I don't mean to pry, but Jim and I would be
happy to know anything we should.

I hope your boys are well. What's the news of them?
Greetings from Jim.

Love,
Pearl

By the time Elizabeth had finished the letter she had also
finished her tea. Her hands had limbered up in the warmth
of the kitchen, and she decided to reply to Pearl right away.
She fetched a notecard from her desk and returned to the
kitchen table. It was a small card, with *The Peaceable Kingdom* printed on the front. Elizabeth thought a brief reply to
her sister-in-law might be for the best and the card was
ideally suited for such. She wrote:

Dear Pearl,

Thank you for your letter. It is always good to hear
from you. Perhaps you and Jim can come up to Boston next Fourth of July. I'd be glad to have you here
at Concord Avenue.

I see Sarah occasionally at Meeting and recently
had one serious conversation with her, at her initia-
tive. I think it's too early to say what will happen with
Sarah and Steven. I can certainly understand your

concern. It continues to look like neither of my boys will be Friends. Mark is simply not religious and, as you know, Andrew went away to college and came back an Episcopalian. And that means there's no help of Quaker grandchildren on the Elliot side of the family. But these things are in God's hands. Perhaps some of our kids are called to the Society and some are not.

Let's hope Sarah goes where she is led. I pray that she will.

Love,
Elizabeth

Elizabeth looked back over the card and wondered if she should have responded more sympathetically or at greater length. Arthritis pain in her right hand, however, decided her against any further attempts at family responsibility for the day. She sealed up the envelope.

7

And this is the Comfort of the Good,
that the Grave cannot hold them,
and that they live as soon as they die.
For Death is no more
than the turning of us over from time to eternity.
Death, then, being the way and condition of life,
we cannot love to live,
if we cannot bear to die.

> *William Penn, seventeenth-century Quaker and*
> *founder of Pennsylvania*

Sunday was a rainy and arthritic day. Elizabeth was in pain from the moment she awoke. She went to Meeting, glad to have company other than her aching joints. As the worship hour began she recited the Twenty-third Psalm, but her mind drifted away into questions about John Hoffman's life before she reached "my cup runneth over." The Clerk tried to clear her mind of murder and joint pain, but could not focus on prayer, despite her best efforts. By the end of the hour she gave up, content to be with Friends and support their efforts to worship by her presence. Near the close of worship a student rose to speak about the blessings she experienced as a soup-kitchen volunteer and related her work to Jesus's Sermon on the Mount. The words were simple and few and reminded Elizabeth that her own problems were not the only ones being faced in Cambridge this First-day.

Harriet Parker had care of Meeting, and she closed the worship by shaking hands with her neighbors. Other Friends followed her example. Announcements about the upcoming week were made, and then the Meetinghouse filled with sound as people rose to leave and chatted with everyone around. Elizabeth saw her niece in the far corner of the room and moved slowly through the crowd to greet her.

From nowhere in particular, Neil Stevenson materialized at Elizabeth's elbow. "Good morning, Friend. I hope your car troubles have been fixed."

"Yes, my dear son the engineer went to Arlington and took it to a garage nearby. They put in a new water pump, just as you predicted. It's running fine now, I'm happy to say."

Sarah had seen her aunt when she first began her journey through the Meetinghouse throng. Sarah was alone and came up, smiling, to her aunt.

Elizabeth introduced Neil to her niece.

"Pleased to meet you," said the student. "And it's good to see you, Aunt. I just wanted to say hello, but I've got to run off right away. I've got two problem sets due tomorrow that I've got to get cracking on."

Sarah departed, but to Elizabeth's surprise, Neil made no move to go. He asked if she were staying for lunch. Elizabeth often did not want to stay; today she could think only of going home to another dose of arthritis medicine and retiring to a hot bath. She made her excuses as gently as she could. Neil was not Hugo Coleman, after all. She did not want him to go away, but this was not the day to spend time with him.

The rest of Sunday and Monday, too, were dominated by arthritis pain for Elizabeth. She was quite discouraged by Monday afternoon. It had proved impossible to raise Tim's high bail. She had spoken to several bail bondsmen, but without a substantial, and nonrefundable, advance, they would not consider the matter. Who would risk a lot of money on the conduct of a disturbed homeless man? Elizabeth knew that Friends Meeting would not consider putting up the money. It had an endowment fund sufficient to meet the bail, but she had known Hugo Coleman to dig in his heels at trifling sums and small risks. Tim's conduct in the future could not be predicted by anyone, and even Friends like Adam might feel hesitant about putting up bail for him.

Elizabeth still did not know if Detective Burnham's conduct at the police station had been illegal. She had called the ACLU on Thursday and again on Friday. Only on Monday did a lawyer return her calls. The lawyer said he thought it sounded as if Detective Burnham's actions had been a clear violation of the law, but that he could do nothing on the matter until the following week because he was in court each day on a major pornography case.

On Tuesday the skies cleared, the temperature went up, and Elizabeth awoke with more energy. She systematically did her housework and her laundry, glad for the strength to scrub and wash. As she worked, she thought through everything she knew about John Hoffman and those who knew him. But the more she thought about the matter, the more she realized that at least one good Quaker must be guilty of terrible misconduct. It was a sobering day.

She awakened Wednesday morning with a heavy sense of depression and only roused herself out of bed by an act of will. What had seemed sobering yesterday now was becoming a burden. Her arthritis pain was back, and she struggled to slowly bend and flex enough to dress. Sitting in her kitchen with a double dose of arthritis medicine and a little breakfast in her stomach, she drank a cup of strong tea. Her doctor had recommended to her that she limit her caffeine consumption. Although she had easily quit coffee, she found that life without tea was bleak. Each day she resolved to drink less, but each day she brewed herself at least a potful. She comforted herself today with the thought that she needed to be alert. To prepare her spirit for the upcoming memorial Meeting, the first of her Clerkship, Elizabeth read through the final part of the journal of John Woolman.

Woolman's courageous life had ended calmly. While preaching in England, he had become gravely ill. Knowing he had smallpox, and seeing death approaching, Woolman enjoyed true confidence and peace. He seemed unafraid of what he was experiencing. Several days before his death he cried out, "O my Father! My Father! How comfortable art thou to my soul in this trying season!" Later he said, "My hope is in Christ . . . I shall be gathered to my everlasting rest." He gave instructions to one of the women with him about wrapping his corpse in cheap flannel; she wept. Woolman said to her, "I had rather thou wouldst guard against weeping and sorrowing for me, my sister. I sorrow not. I look at the face of my dear Redeemer, for sweet is his voice and his countenance comely."

As Elizabeth sat at her kitchen table she recalled her husband's death, six years ago. He had suffered greatly from cancer and from pain induced by the medical treatments for his condition. She did, however, remember the memorial Meeting for her husband, Michael, as being a time of joyful worship and thanksgiving for what his rich life had been. But the memorial for John Hoffman would be different. Although there could and should be joy and thanks in it, it would be marred by the nature of his death. As far as Elizabeth knew, a murdered Quaker was unprecedented in modern New England history.

Elizabeth's thoughts were interrupted by a telephone call from Erik Swensen. He explained that he had found a thoughtful letter he had received from John when Erik had been hospitalized for exploratory surgery several years previously. John's letter, Erik said, reflected his generous and empathetic nature so clearly that it seemed appropriate to read a portion of it at the upcoming memorial Meeting. Erik asked Elizabeth if she would care to hear it. She explained again, as gently as she could, that Quaker Meetings took place in silence and that although someone might speak in the context of that silence, such speech was spontaneous and not planned ahead of time. Reading something in a Meeting was permitted in the Quaker understanding of worship only if the Spirit spontaneously called a person to read. Such readings could therefore not be planned ahead of the event. Erik seemed puzzled and asked if he was welcome at the meeting. She tried to make it clear to him that he was indeed welcome, but would not be welcome to read anything decided on ahead of the Meeting.

"By the way," said Elizabeth, "several people in our congregation have been asked by the police to explain where they were on the Monday afternoon when John was killed. I suppose you've been questioned also?"

"Yes," replied Erik, clearly not offended by the query. "It's a good thing for me that some people can say where I was. I'd come into work as usual. John always took Monday holidays off, but I don't. The staff was out also because of Columbus Day. In the afternoon I was looking for some papers which should've been on my desk, or possibly Muriel's desk, and when I couldn't find them I called her at home to ask where they were. She said they were filed in my office, but when I looked, I still couldn't find them. So I called her back—we got rather chippy at each other, I am afraid—and she said it was possible they were in John's office. I was sure they wouldn't be there, but I let myself in and searched there. There was no sign of them. Then, just by chance, I did find them, in Muriel's Out basket. So it goes to show that competent help make their share of mistakes, too."

"Are you sure enough of the time of those phone calls to be able to tell the police?" asked Elizabeth.

"Oh, yes," replied Erik. "It was just at three P.M. when I first called her; the second call would have been shortly after that. Anyway, the papers didn't give me the figures I needed, and I was in a pretty foul mood and all, so I called it a day and went to my favorite watering hole. A place called Mike's, not far from here. Mike and the boys can vouch for me for the rest of the day. In the end my wife came and gave me a ride home. The police have already talked to her to check that out."

Elizabeth supposed that Erik had drunk a lot. Barring going to Mike's herself, a distasteful thought, she didn't see there was much she could do to check Erik's story. She once again said she looked forward to Erik's presence at the memorial, and then she and Erik said good-bye.

The rest of the week passed uneventfully as far as the murder case was concerned. Elizabeth was called on to take care of her grandson, Nicky, on both Thursday and Friday when his usual day-care arrangements fell through. So many of the children in the day care he attended had chicken pox that the adults in charge decided to close for a week. Since both of Nicky's parents worked full time, Grandma Elizabeth stepped in. She loved her grandson enormously, but by Friday afternoon she was ready to drop. Her exhaustion after two days with an eighteen-month-old was deep. On Friday night she slept more soundly than she had for months.

Saturday dawned clear and bright. The dry weather had limbered up Elizabeth's joints during the night, and she got out of bed with only minor stiffness. A hot shower and dressing herself were pleasures this morning, rather than the burdens they were sometimes becoming. She went downstairs and saw no sign of the cat. Because of the ever-cooler weather, a number of finches were at the bird feeder as she ate her breakfast. She felt good about the day and the service scheduled for eleven o'clock. Her reading from Woolman seemed to have helped her in considering the memorial.

When Elizabeth arrived at the Friends' Meetinghouse,

she saw a police car parked out front. Near it stood Detective Burnham, hands in his coat pockets. She had spoken to him on the telephone during the week, giving him the results of her visit to the Salvation Army. As she had suspected, he did not admit that her work had any value and merely said his people would check into it when they had time. For an instant, Elizabeth wondered if he had come to observe the other people who were involved in the case. She imagined, however, that such a self-confident man as Burnham still believed he held the right man in custody. She approached Burnham, said hello, and asked if he had been able to follow up the Salvation Army information.

"Not yet," answered the detective. "I just haven't had time to do anything on the Hoffman case because of two other homicides that've come up. But I'll talk to the Salvation Army on Monday. That's a promise."

Elizabeth then asked if he intended to attend the memorial Meeting.

"Yes," answered Burnham. "I had hoped to attend, that is, if non-Quakers are allowed."

"Quakers and non-Quakers alike are welcome at all Friends gatherings," answered Elizabeth, "although most Friends would appreciate it if you remain silent during the Meeting."

"Oh, of course!" answered Burnham. "I'm here just to note the death of the victim in a formal way. It helps me remember what this job is about. The deaths that the homicide department sees are usually a lot grubbier than this Hoffman case, and sometimes I get pretty burned out. Funerals remind me that my job has a point. The victim has a right to see justice done, after all."

"Perhaps that's so," answered Elizabeth. "The problem is how to understand justice. I'm sure that John Hoffman wouldn't want retribution to be in our thinking today. Notions of retribution have no place in Quaker life."

"It's not retribution I'm after," answered Burnham. "It's justice. In a case of cold-blooded murder like this, surely the idea of justice is not so complex."

The two had been walking slowly toward the door as they spoke. When they arrived, Elizabeth motioned for the detective to be silent. She took his coat from him and hung it up on the long coat rack in the foyer. She then motioned for Detective Burnham to precede her into the Meetinghouse proper. This he did, rather awkwardly, as he always preferred women to precede him through doorways. He sat down on the first available bench.

Elizabeth entered the Meetinghouse and saw it was already nearly full. A large number of Quakers and other people as well had gathered to celebrate John Hoffman's life. She saw Muriel Taylor, John's accountant and secretary, and near her, Erik Swensen. Muriel looked pale but at ease. She was alert and looking around with apparent interest. Erik was dressed in a conservative suit and sat stiffly erect. He stared vacantly ahead. Thomas Hoffman, John's distant relative whom Elizabeth had met at the reading of John's will, was also present. He sat on a bench at the end of the Meetinghouse. Bill Hoffman, in a charcoal-gray suit, sat next to him. Bill nodded almost imperceptibly at Elizabeth as she came in. She bowed her head slightly as she made her way to a still-empty bench.

Elizabeth tried to concentrate on the worship and put her suspicions aside. She told herself that she should not think about John's death, as such. The Meeting had been called, after all, to commemorate a long and rich life. But it was impossible not to remember that Tim Schouweiler sat in police custody. She thought that Tim would have been here today, had he been free.

Under the circumstances, it was a great challenge to leave the outcome of the murder investigation solely in the hands of God. Elizabeth no longer considered leaving the matter in the hands of the police. As she sat on the hard bench her mind drifted into worry about Tim. What was happening to him? She was determined to do what she could to help Tim, and she was deeply angry at someone in this room. Someone, after all, was guilty of the killing and also of denial.

Anger was not a common experience for Elizabeth Elliot. She disliked it. Surrounded by the Meetinghouse silence, she wondered if the anger of prophets like Isaiah and Amos of the Old Testament might have felt like this. She stopped herself and thought again. Did her anger differ much from Detective Burnham's idea of the victim's death demanding some sort of justice? Perhaps she and the detective had more in common than she might like to think. But the police and Burnham aimed to forcibly punish someone in this room. Retribution and punishment were not Elizabeth's goals. But perhaps she and Burnham did have a sense of outrage in common. She set these ideas aside and shifted forward slightly as she looked around the room.

The Meeting was, of course, silent. At least, silence is at the base of the memorial Meeting as understood by Quakers. However, many people may speak at such meetings, as at Quaker weddings. For someone of John Hoffman's age, had he not been murdered, there might have been an element of joy as well as loss in this memorial Meeting. Had his death been natural, it might have been possible to see the fullness of his life. He had, to all outward appearances, lived a demanding and successful life. He had been an able man, and he had always been generous toward Friends in any trouble or need. Many members of this Meeting had good reason to rejoice in the life and work of John Hoffman.

But the fact of murder hung over the assemblage.

Through one of the tall windows on the east side of the room, Elizabeth saw Adam Chrisler bicycle into the yard. He stooped to lock his bike to a sapling, as she had often seen him do. Adam was one of the sturdy Quakers who did not own a car, but always biked or took public transportation on principle.

Elizabeth lost herself in thinking of Tim again, but then saw that Adam had come in. He had seated himself in Tim's habitual place. Adam wore a black turtleneck sweater under a worn blazer. It struck her as regrettable that he had not put on a suit and tie for such a somber Meeting. Adam had known John personally, after all, and she thought some token of respect was not too much to ask, even from younger people. She almost shook her head in disapprobation but caught herself just in time. She looked down at the floor, thinking uncharitable things about the unfortunate influence the 1960s had had on Meeting life. Again she stopped herself and asked herself if such a strong reaction against a good Friend was really warranted.

She looked up at Adam and wondered why she felt unease about his slightly countercultural life-style. Adam was a longtime member of Meeting, after all, and in many ways his life reflected the virtues of simplicity and integrity that Quakers so often preached. She should be less distrustful of the young, she told herself, and more trustful of those whose clothes and hair reflected modern trends.

The stillness grew deeper and, for the knowing, unvoiced prayer filled the room. Then, one by one, some of the older Quakers rose and spoke quietly about John's life and all that he had given to the Meeting over forty years. The words were simple and true. Toward the end of an hour, the Clerk was finally able to sink into prayer herself. The quiet enveloped her in warmth, and she felt a peace that had been absent since John's death. She settled further into this feeling, and the warmth increased within her. She stopped thinking in words and ideas and reached out for a sense of direct communion. She was not disappointed.

Emerging by degrees from prayer, Elizabeth decided the Meeting had come to its natural end. She turned to her neighbor and shook hands. After this silent closing of worship, Friends and others present rose and slowly began to file out of the Meetinghouse. Erik Swensen, now looking ashen, remained seated longer than most, as did Adam. But Elizabeth decided not to speak to them within the silence which they might wish to prolong, so she moved toward the door. She found herself next to Muriel Taylor, John and Erik's secretary.

"Thank you for letting us all come," said Muriel quietly. "I appreciate your letting outsiders be a part of this. It was beautiful."

"You are welcome here, of course. We're glad you could come."

"Perhaps I should stay," said Muriel, as she stopped next to the Meetinghouse door, "and speak to Erik as he comes out. I think I should say hello."

"He doesn't look well."

"He's in for worse," answered Muriel. "Yesterday he learned he is under investigation for banking fraud. I'm glad I gave notice last week. I can be out of the office by the time the indictments are handed down."

"Is it that bad, then?" asked Elizabeth.

"Yes, I'm afraid it is. Apparently there were a number of things Erik had going on the side, as well as what I knew about. The savings and loan deregulation changed a lot of things for us. Erik was getting money from every S and L in the state, rolling over loans with newly borrowed money. A little of the partnership money was going into it, too— that was the part I knew about—but mostly he was in this on his own. He has lost everything now.

"It's all very sad, not only for Erik but also for me and everyone associated with him. In a way it's good that John died when he did; he's been spared seeing what is coming down the tracks at the partnership and especially at Erik."

Elizabeth offered her sympathy and then said, "I spoke to Erik about where he was the afternoon of Columbus Day, and he said he had called you a couple of times from work. I was wondering if you recall the phone calls and when they were?"

"Oh, yes, I remember them. He was upset, and I thought at the time that he must be alone at work and already hitting the bottle. He wanted to know where certain papers he'd been working on were, and he thought I should be able to say exactly where to find them, holiday or no holiday.

"There were at least two phone calls, the last one pretty angry on both sides, I'm sorry to say, and they were just after three. My favorite soap had just come on the TV. Usually I tape it with a VCR because I'm at work. Then I watch it when I get home. But since I was home on Columbus Day, I'd turned the VCR off. I didn't want to speak to Erik while the program was on the tube. It's sort of embarrassing for a supposedly educated person like myself to admit that a soap is so important to me, but we all have our quirks and I hate to miss a show."

"I see," said Elizabeth. "Erik also mentioned that he went from work to a bar named Mike's. He said it was a pretty common practice of his."

"Recently he's been going there almost daily," responded Muriel. "As I said to you earlier, it's not a good period in his life, and he's been hitting the sauce. I'm sure that's what's made some of his behavior, and his decisions, erratic. Mike's is where his current wife often finds him, I know. At night, I mean, to bring him home."

Elizabeth saw that Erik was nearing the door, so she nodded in his direction as a warning to Muriel and said, "You and Erik will find coffee in the Friends' Center next door if you wish."

Muriel thanked her and moved on to say a few words to Erik. Elizabeth reentered the Meetinghouse to see if Adam was still there.

He was sitting just as he had been when the Meeting closed. He was hunched up and leaning over his knees. She sat beside him and waited in silence.

After a few minutes Adam sat up straighter and sighed. He slowly looked to his left, where Elizabeth sat, and she thought he looked very pale. The black turtleneck which he was wearing set off his face, making it look pasty and bloodless.

"You don't look well, Adam," said Elizabeth. "Perhaps this is not a good time to speak, but I only meant to say hello and ask how you're doing."

"Thanks, Friend," replied Adam. "I'm feeling bad. No sleep this week, that's all." No one else was left in the room except Elizabeth and Adam, and she wondered if he intended to stay and pray alone here. Thinking that likely, she rose to go, but hearing her movement, Adam looked up and quickly said, "Please stay a moment if you can. It's a hard time for me."

Elizabeth sat down again and waited in silence.

"John Hoffman and I spent a lot of time together this past year, Friend, more than you might guess. John began a study of liberation theology last winter and asked me to join him in reading some of Sobrino's books. All of liberation theology looks at the gospel from the perspective of those who've been excluded from power and from economic success. It really took hold of John. We met each week in Harvard Square for supper and discussion of what we were reading together."

Adam paused. Elizabeth, to whom this information was all new, waited silently to see if he had more to say.

"John got to know Tim a bit last year, too," continued Adam, "and Tim used to stop by and do a little yard work for him. Just a little contact with Tim, with someone alive and real and in the gutter, changed John's thinking about poverty."

"Yes, Tim told me recently that he knew John, and I must say I was a bit surprised. John always seemed so wrapped up in his business and Quaker committee work. Spending time with Tim must have been a real change," said Elizabeth.

"But the wonderful thing about John was the growth and change that was going on within him this year! Elizabeth, I'm not sure that anyone in Meeting knew what was happening to John, except me. He was a very private man. The whole structure of liberation theology began to change him. I've never seen anyone so old and set in his ways become so energized and renewed.

"He had been talking about changing his life this fall. He only spoke in vague terms to me, but I gather he meant to give up his work. The business deals seemed to have lost their old appeal. He seemed more and more free to me. It was wonderfully moving to see, even though he didn't explain very much of it. All that growth has been cut off now, all of it wasted forever."

"No, Friend," replied Elizabeth. "Nothing of growth toward God's will is wasted. I'm sorry that John has been killed, and I'm angry about it also, but neither his life nor anything which was happening to him recently was a waste. I'm sure of that."

"Your faith runs deeper than mine!" said Adam and buried his head in his hands. He began to sob softly. Elizabeth leaned forward to pray for him in his grief.

When Adam had recovered and left on his bike, Elizabeth locked up the Meetinghouse proper and went next door. The modest reception after the Meeting had broken up and few Friends remained. Most Quakers don't linger after memorial services, either because they have learned to accept death as part of life or because they have not reached that stage of maturity and instead find themselves quite uncomfortable at any kind of funeral. But in the kitchen several Friends were chatting and sipping coffee. Elizabeth greeted everyone, declined coffee and herb tea, and began to hunt through the kitchen cupboards for proper tea. Tom Redburn stepped forward to help her and soon found a small box of Earl Grey tea bags.

"Thanks very much," said Elizabeth, accepting the box from Tom's hand. She found a cup and made stout tea from the pot of hot water left from the reception. Turning again toward Tom, she said, "I'm glad to see you here today. I know you are a friend of Bill Hoffman's and I'm sure this must be a difficult time for him."

"Yes, I think it is," he answered, "and unfortunately Bill isn't able to express his feelings very well. I worry about him quite a bit these days."

"He is quite self-contained, isn't he?" answered Elizabeth, sipping tea. "I'm sure it must be a real stress dealing with the police and their questions. Bill mentioned to me that he met you on the afternoon his uncle died, but he seemed to feel that you couldn't vouch for him except for a short period of time."

"That's right," responded Tom. "He and I had a beer at The Station in Central Square—it must have been about four in the afternoon—but he left immediately. He always has too much work to do, between his sixty-five-hour work weeks and all the committee work he does for us here."

"It's a shame he doesn't have an alibi for the whole afternoon, of course," said Elizabeth, "but I don't think the police are focusing on Bill."

"No," said Tom. "The cops have picked up one of the street people, haven't they?"

"Yes, that's true," answered Elizabeth. "He's a man named Tim Schouweiler. He comes here every Sunday. But he's not guilty and that will soon be established."

Jean Nyman and Hugo Coleman were in one corner of the kitchen, and Elizabeth stepped over to them. Jean lived at the Beacon Hill Friends House in Boston, where Adam reported he had gone after the protest demonstration. Elizabeth chatted with both Jean and Hugo until, mercifully, Patience Silverstone took Hugo aside to discuss something more privately. Seeing her chance, Elizabeth expressed her concern for Adam and her dismay about how poor he looked today. She then asked Jean about the day of John's death.

"Yes," said Jean, "of course I remember Columbus Day. Several Friends came to supper at the house after the demonstration was over. Adam and I ate together and discussed the Gulf."

"Do you know when Adam arrived? The police may ask you that, you see," responded Elizabeth.

"No, not really." Jean paused and thought. Then she continued firmly, "Supper begins about six. I can't say exactly what happened that day, but sometime around six I came down, saw Adam, and we fell into our usual arguments about how to resist the Pentagon. But I remember Adam said he'd come straight from the demonstration. He was hoarse from chanting outside city hall all afternoon."

"I see," said Elizabeth. Just then Hugo made a move to break away from Patience. Elizabeth decided it was best to say good-bye to Jean. She washed her cup and returned it to its proper shelf. Then she said good-bye to everyone, reminding them to lock the door as they left.

8

Prayer, then, is communion, whether it takes the form of petition, intercession, thanksgiving, or whether it be just the quiet unveiling of the heart to a trusted friend, the outpouring of the soul to the one who is nearest of all.

William Littleboy, 1937

Despite beautiful fall weather, the Sunday crowd at the Meetinghouse had been thick. Not many Cambridge Quakers, it seemed, were driving in the hills of New Hampshire, enjoying the fall colors. The thought of a color drive had been in Elizabeth's mind when she got up that morning, but the responsibilities of a Clerk did not allow for absences on Sundays. She contented herself with giving an extra handful of seed to her juncos and finches. Then, as a treat for herself, she walked to Meeting via Harvard Square where she purchased a sweet roll to go. She was finishing her roll and feeling upbeat when she got to Longfellow Park. The sight of the Meetinghouse, however, dampened her spirits. Her mind returned to the events surrounding John's death.

Elizabeth was glad she did not have care of Meeting for Worship. She could journey through the worshipful silence without immediate feelings of responsibility today. The atmosphere of the Meeting was reserved. The silence still carried much of the mood of a memorial. Elizabeth had trouble capturing the deep peace and warmth she had found in yesterday's prayer. Time passed slowly.

Worship was also a trial, in a different way, for another person in the Meetinghouse. Young Jack Nelson labored on his own through the silence. He was oblivious of any difficulties the adults around him might be having with prayer. He had brought a small Match Box toy to Meeting with him. As long as he played with it quietly on his legs, his mother made no objection to his activities. The toy was his favorite: a red pickup truck with a tailgate that opened and a clear plastic windshield.

After a few minutes, Jack cautiously propelled the truck across the back of the bench in front of him. The sound of the wheels turning on the wood was enough to bring down his mother's censure. He was still for a minute, gripping the truck in both hands, but soon he began to play with the pickup on his legs once again. Suddenly, for no reason discernible to Jack, the pickup truck dove off the edge of his bench toward the floor. It made a surprisingly loud and sharp report on impact. Even as Jack's mother was reaching to grab him, Jack's small and lithe body followed the path the truck had taken. Her hand just missed him as he dropped to the floor and crawled to the truck, now sitting quietly under the bench in front of the one the Nelsons occupied.

"Jack!" his mother hissed. "Come back up here!"

Jack dropped to his belly, reached for the pickup with his right hand, and retrieved it. He instantly returned to his place, unfortunately kicking his bench loudly with his left shoe.

Knowing his mother as he did, Jack had the pickup firmly clasped in his right hand when he crawled up beside her. He feared confiscation, and given his mother's thoughts at the moment, his fear was justified. But Alice Nelson, seeing her son's tightly balled fist, decided against direct action. The Nelsons had caused enough noise, she reasoned, without starting open warfare in the Meetinghouse.

After a minute passed without maternal action, Jack cautiously relaxed his grip on the truck. He held it in both hands near his face and examined it carefully. Half of the pickup's windshield was gone. It had cracked down the middle, and half of it was not to be seen. Even the part of the windshield that remained was scarred by impact.

Jack sniffed. It was his most valued Match Box toy, the one he prized above all others. He began to cry as he contemplated his bleak future. His mother, responding to the sniffling, put her arm around her boy's shoulders, dropped her head to his level, and whispered, "What's wrong?"

Jack mutely held up the pickup for her to see. She reached over with her left hand to take the offered truck, which looked its normal self to her adult eyes. She thought Jack was overcome by his transgression and was offering the toy that had caused the noise to his mother as a gesture of repentance. She put the toy into her purse, which lay on the bench on her left, away from Jack.

Jack was horrified to see the truck disappear. He had asked for sympathy and instead of receiving it, he had been deprived of what small comfort he had in the Meeting-house. His sniffling turned to a wail of despair.

Alice Nelson, mystified and exasperated, stood up and dragged her son to his feet. She began to pull him toward the door. Jack, knowing that being led out of the Meeting-house would mean he was in deep trouble, shouted, "No! No! Mama, no!"

He was pronouncing a second sentence full of "no's" when the Nelsons disappeared out the door of the worship room.

Elizabeth had heard the crash of the pickup truck to the floor, but had not followed the events thereafter until Alice Nelson led her boy outside. Elizabeth could not remember the boy's name, and since the incident did not concern her she quickly returned to prayer. She began to find some peace in the silence and slipped gladly into the spirit of one of the psalms that she knew by heart. The rest of the hour of worship went by, not without profit for those in atten-dance, and Neil Stevenson closed the Meeting by shaking hands with all around him. Jane Thompson then made announcements about the coming week. As frequently was the case, many Friends were reticent immediately after Meeting. But a few moments of release from the Meetinghouse itself seemed to alter everyone's spirits. Lunch was loud and chaotic, as usual. Adam Chrisler, in the kitchen, ladled out soup for all comers. In contrast to yesterday, he seemed composed. Bill Hoffman spoke briefly to Elizabeth as she tasted her soup, thanking her for organizing the memorial Meeting. He looked more relaxed than Elizabeth had seen him since his uncle's death.

As some Friends finished their lunch and others worked to clean the kitchen, Elizabeth left and crossed the alleyway to the Meetinghouse proper. In the bright October sun, Alice Nelson was standing on the steps, hands on her hips.

"Don't be a pest, Jack. I'm speaking to Mrs. Thompson."

Jack turned away from his mother and Jane Thompson as Elizabeth watched him. The adults returned to their conversation and the Clerk walked halfway toward the boy.

"Good afternoon, Master Nelson," said Elizabeth with a smile.

"What you call me that for?" asked the boy suspiciously.

"They used to call boys that, a long time ago. And I'm afraid I don't know your first name."

"I'm Jack."

"And I'm Elizabeth Elliot. When I was your age, I had lots of trouble sitting through Meeting for Worship. It's not easy, I know. But when you grow up, the time inside the Meetinghouse goes by differently."

Alice, now done speaking to Jane, stepped over to her son.

"We're sorry for the disturbance this morning, Friend."

"I wasn't disturbed," replied Elizabeth, "and I remember what a labor it can be to remain quiet for an hour or more."

"But it's a skill Quaker boys need to learn," said Alice firmly.

Jack, still smarting from what his mother had said about him being "impossible" when she had removed him from the Meetinghouse, could no longer restrain his temper.

"Quakers aren't always quiet!" he said stridently. "Remember those two men I told you about last time we were here!"

"Quakers are always quiet on Sundays. What two men are you talking about?" asked Alice distractedly.

"The two men who were over there," said Jack, waving at Longfellow Park. "The ones who were shouting at each other."

"If you mean homeless men," said Alice, "you know they don't count as Quakers even if they come to Meeting."

"No, no! Not homeless men! Quakers!"

Elizabeth, remembering her niece's report about an argument including John Hoffman, looked seriously at Jack.

"Could you show me where the men were when they shouted at each other?"

Jack was delighted by her interest. He skipped down the walk and turned into the park, as Elizabeth and a reluctant Alice followed.

"It was down here," said Jack happily, pointing down a flight of steps at the end of the park toward the statue of Mr. Longfellow.

Elizabeth looked behind her. Only the corner of the Meetinghouse could be seen. The rest of Quaker property was effectively screened from this part of Longfellow Park.

"Did you hear what the men were saying?" she asked Jack.

"No. They were angry and I ran away. The old man's face was all red."

"Which old man was it?"

"I don't know."

"Do you know who the other man was?"

Jack suddenly became shy. He had not expected this much interest in his story. He slipped over to his mother and took hold of her hand. He shook his head.

"I see," said Elizabeth. She smiled at Alice and added, "I heard earlier about the argument here and was curious as to who might have been involved." She turned toward Jack, who was becoming more relaxed as he clung to his mother. "Thank you for showing me the place."

"Whatever Quakers do in the park, Jack," said Alice in stern tones, "we are always quiet in the Meetinghouse. But it's time to go home now."

The three of them turned and walked up the park sidewalk, Elizabeth lost in thought. She said good-bye and then went back to the Meetinghouse as the Nelsons departed for home.

Elizabeth walked to the Clerk's bench at the head of the Meetinghouse, trying to compose her thoughts. She had called for a special Business Meeting this afternoon to consider the bequest that John's will had left Friends. As she wrestled with her ideas, Elizabeth realized that the burdens of the Clerkship were weighing her down. Sitting on the Clerk's bench, she noted that her head felt heavy and there was a pain in the back of her skull. Could it be from too much Clerking, or might it be a side effect of the new blood pressure medication? She sighed, trying to ignore the headache and collect herself.

Other Friends came back into the room, and the Business Meeting began in silence. Elizabeth let the silence continue as a few tardy Friends arrived, bustling to their places, and let it continue through some fidgeting of three high-schoolers sitting in the back. Finally, when true silence was achieved, she prayed briefly. At the end of her silent prayer she looked up, welcomed Friends to the Meeting, and read a short passage from one of the letters of George Fox on the topic of stewardship. She then put before Friends the subject of the $100,000 gift from John Hoffman's estate and asked for silence-based discussion concerning whether to accept it and what to do with it.

Hugo Coleman was the first to speak, no surprise to anyone. He rose and stood near the room's center, dressed in a natty sports coat and corduroys. Elizabeth tried to resist the feelings of dislike which threatened to well up in her. Between her headache and her long-term problems with Hugo, she felt rather overwhelmed for a moment.

Hugo gave a long speech explaining that the Meeting was behind on its budget for the fiscal year, more behind than usual. He reminded Friends that the new furnace had cost a great deal and that unless all Friends increased their giving, the purchase of the furnace endangered the financial solvency of the Meeting. He finished by saying that in light of the needs of the Quaker community, and the fact that John's bequest was unrestricted, the money should go immediately into general operating funds. Any money left over at the end of the fiscal year could go into the endowment fund.

A few minutes after Hugo had resumed his seat, Patience Silverstone rose. She looked all eighty-five of her years this afternoon, but she stood straight and looked sharply around the Meetinghouse. With a vigorous voice she spoke about the need for stewardship, but also the need for generosity.

"We're always behind on our annual budget, Friends. That's nothing new, and we always make it up at the end of the calendar year, when people contribute for tax-deduction purposes. Or at worst, we get caught up at the end of the fiscal year, when Friends pull together to fulfill the budget plans. We should go ahead in the faith that the same will be the case again."

Patience went on to propose that the Meeting divide this substantial and unexpected gift in two, giving half to a Quaker project that was building low-income housing in Boston and half to the Meeting's fund for indigent Friends.

Wally Orvick, a member of the Finance Committee and the right-hand man of Hugo Coleman, immediately rose to place his weight against this proposal. He gave the exact figures of the Meeting's bank balance, reiterated that the Meeting was farther behind in the fiscal year budget than it had ever been before, and said he hoped that Friends would remember that money to meet the operating budget must come from somewhere. If the members did not substantially increase their giving, he lectured, then John Hoffman's bequest was absolutely needed in the general operating funds.

At this point in the discussion, Elizabeth called for silence. She could see that the spirit of listening and cooperation was absent. She reminded Friends that unless every person present was willing to listen to the Spirit, Quaker decision making could not work.

After a few minutes, the silence was broken by Adam Chrisler. He got to his feet slowly and looked around the gathering. Running his hands through his hair, he cleared his throat and said, "Friends, we don't understand the circumstances around John Hoffman's death. But we do know that he didn't die naturally."

Adam paused as his words sank in. Elizabeth looked at him closely and noted the small signs of exhaustion in his face. He looked more careworn than he had at lunchtime. Perhaps he had had some sleep last night, as she had thought, but clearly he still felt the strain of recent events.

Adam continued calmly without the hoarseness that had recently been troubling him. "In these circumstances, I don't think we should accept a gift which is ours because of violence. Our pacifist testimony is a strong one. It's our testimony best known to the world. We need to think about what Quakers stand for. Let's consider giving all of this gift away, to one of the housing projects in East Cambridge, for example, but certainly not retaining any of it within the Quaker community. The money is falling into our hands due to a killing, and Friends, I'm sure, don't want to profit in any way from violence."

Adam sat down heavily. The silence of the Meeting was deep and steady. Elizabeth let it continue for as long as the Spirit moved. She prayerfully considered all that had been said, trying to consider in her heart even what Hugo had been called to say. As she sat in the Clerk's chair, she realized that she herself had additional reservations about this money, beyond what Patience and Adam had voiced. She knew John's thinking about how to use his wealth had been changing just before his death. If he had lived a few more days, wouldn't he have revised his will and promptly "divested" himself of his wealth? With his new ideas about his finances, the Meeting might have received a token amount from him, 1 percent of the residue. Surely this was a different notion of stewardship than shown in the will that Bill Hoffman was presenting to the world as his uncle's final wishes.

The silence continued. Elizabeth rested her heavy head on her hand. She thought it likely that John had spoken to Bill on the day before his death, after Sunday morning

Meeting for Worship. Bill might not have had time to make the legal changes that John had asked for, but should the Meeting accept what was legally, but not morally, its due? And the possibility must be faced that Bill, fearful of losing his inheritance, had gone to his uncle's house on Monday afternoon, argued with him, and hit him over the head in the heat of the moment.

The silence continued for a long time, even by Quaker standards. Finally, Hugo Coleman was on his feet again. He cleared his throat and spoke, but he spoke more softly than when he had first explained his views.

"Friends," he began, "our own needs are great. But what Adam Chrisler has said carries weight with me. I had not thought of things that way. But I again repeat that John Hoffman would have been pleased to have us spend the money in any way we deemed necessary. That is what an unrestricted gift means. John was a businessman and a longtime member of our community. I'm sure he knew what he was about. He always helped us meet the budget while he was alive. His generous contributions in December and at the end of the fiscal year often kept us in the black. I feel clear that we can accept this money. John would have wanted it that way.

"But as we sit here, I don't feel we are close to making a Spirit-led decision: we need more time to think about what has been said. How would Friends feel about postponing our decision until next week, when we could meet again to address this problem?"

Murmurs of agreement were heard all around. The Clerk was glad that Hugo had spoken. But because the next weekend already had two weddings scheduled for it, it was decided to meet again on Wednesday evening. Between now and Wednesday, Elizabeth asked all present to consider prayerfully the points raised this Sabbath afternoon. The Meeting closed in a moment of silence, and then all stood up and began to make their way to the door.

Elizabeth paused to gather up papers, and as she did Chris Richardson came up to the Clerk's table to speak to her. Chris, a young woman in Meeting and a graduate student, was politically active. Elizabeth quickly recalled that it was she who had been with Adam outside city hall in Boston on Columbus Day.

"I just want to say, Clerk," began Chris, "that we should move slowly on this question. A lot of the old Friends always think of the budget, and what they really want is to be over budget at the end of the year so they can increase the endowment. But I think Adam has a good point about this money coming to us for bad reasons. That should make us stop and think."

The Clerk could not see that Chris was saying anything new. She murmured something about everyone needing to consider this question in prayer before Wednesday evening. Feeling guilty about the harsh attitude she often had toward Adam and the other young people who had no middle-class aspirations, and particularly about her critical thoughts yesterday during the memorial Meeting, she added, "Chris, I know you're a friend of Adam's, and I'd just like to say that although Adam is often at odds with the older and more conservative element in Meeting, we do respect him. I know of all his work in soup kitchens and I applaud that witness. And I have always been impressed by his simple life. Even those of us in the old guard can see and appreciate his work."

Ignoring the pain in her head, Elizabeth continued: "I know he lives humbly, and although I can't say I've chosen that path, I'm more and more impressed that Adam's life is Spirit led." She was a bit surprised she had said so much to a youngster like Chris. To wind up she added, "Even when I was his age I used a car; I'm sure I couldn't have talked myself into bicycling everywhere, the way he does."

Elizabeth was serious in her effort to respect Friends like Adam, even if her own life-style was different. This was something she knew took more work. She thought it good to say things publicly, and she was pleased with herself for saying these things to Chris.

For her part, Chris was impressed. "Thanks for saying that, Elizabeth. Adam really works hard at what he feels led to do. And he certainly is serious about cutting back on material things. I don't own a car either, but I take the bus and the subway even when I'm only going a few blocks. Adam's the only person I know around here who always bikes."

Elizabeth thought quickly. She said, "On Columbus Day, when Adam went to the demonstration in Boston, do you think he would've biked?"

"Of course! I know he did, because I saw him arrive and lock his bike just as the demo started. He always bikes! Some other Quakers own Saabs!"

Chris did not know that her words held any special importance to the Clerk. But Elizabeth was grateful, at times like these, that she drove an old Chevrolet. The car probably was something of a gas hog, and she knew it was consuming oil at a brisk rate, but old clunkers didn't come in for moral condemnation in Quaker circles. Again her mind turned to the automobile question and the several layers of financial and moral questions involved in owning a car. Perhaps it would be better to give the whole thing up. Between the subway and the bus, she could manage, after all. By an act of will, Elizabeth returned her attention to the young woman in front of her and an apparently greater problem.

"Do you happen to recall when Adam left the demonstration?"

Chris looked puzzled and replied, "No, not really. He was there the whole afternoon it seems like. That was a while ago, Elizabeth, why ask?"

With a shake of her head, Elizabeth murmured something about wondering about Adam's safety from suspicion. Chris was clearly puzzled but not offended.

At this point, Hugo Coleman came up, intent on speaking. Chris excused herself, sensing her conversation with the Clerk had perhaps come to an end anyway. Elizabeth was sorry to see her go, leaving Hugo an open field.

"I was wondering if you'd care to join me this Saturday evening. Our Friendly Eights group is meeting at my house for a potluck and we've space for another Friend."

Elizabeth winced. Friendly Eights was a social group within the Meeting that she always avoided.

"No, thank you. You flatter me with the invitation, but I can't accept."

"I'm sorry," responded Hugo. "You have a conflict?"

Elizabeth could not lie to protect Hugo's feelings. She winced inwardly and said, "Thank you, no, Hugo. But I'm sure the evening will be enjoyable."

Even Hugo Coleman had to accept that answer. He said something about hoping to get together another time and said good-bye. Elizabeth sighed and wondered why Neil Stevenson did not ask her to a Friendly Eights group. Again it occurred to her that she could invite Neil over to her house for tea. But then she felt her headache once again and decided she was too old for such doings.

After locking up the Meetinghouse and putting on her

navy-blue coat, she walked home by way of Harvard Square. The day was still fair, and her headache improved as she walked. She bought the Sunday *Globe* and *The New York Times* and labored home under the glut of newsprint. Elizabeth had never subscribed to a newspaper because she often found the news deeply depressing. But she needed a break today and bought the Sunday papers as a treat, intending to read only the Sunday magazines and the book reviews.

Arriving home, she settled in the kitchen with her treasure, promising the cat she would be fed later in the afternoon and glancing out the window at the bird feeder to make sure it was filled. She decided to begin with the *Boston Globe.* She started to open the paper, which she had carried under the *Times,* but stopped abruptly. On the bottom of the front page was a picture of Erik Swensen, appearing beneath the headline "Suicide in S and L Scandal, page 11." Elizabeth immediately turned to the story and read that Erik K. Swensen, a well-known real estate developer of the partnership of Hoffman and Swensen, had been found dead late Saturday afternoon in his office. He had been shot in the head and a revolver, registered in his name, was lying beside him. A long suicide note was also found with him, the paper said. The contents of the note were not revealed beyond the statement that the deceased admitted to fraud and feared the consequences of the investigation now underway by federal authorities. The paper reported that Swensen's body had been found by his secretary. The police did not suspect foul play.

Elizabeth sat quietly at her kitchen table for several minutes taking in this death. Birds came and went outside the kitchen window at her feeder as she sat absorbing this additional piece of tragic news. Sparkle leapt up on her lap, and she stroked the cat absentmindedly. Without any discernible cause, the cat took fright and fled to the safety of the basement. Elizabeth sighed. After a few minutes, she fetched the telephone book for the western suburbs, found an M. L. Taylor listed in Lexington, and dialed. Muriel was at home, and although she was startled to hear from Elizabeth, she quickly made it clear she wanted to talk.

"After your memorial service yesterday," said Muriel, "I stopped in Harvard Square to do some errands. Then I went to our office to finish some work. The next week is my last before quitting, you see, and I wanted the place as shipshape as I can make it. I've been going through John's files and trying to make it clear to Erik where everything is kept. This weekend I thought I'd better clean out my own office and make sure that everything there was organized.

"When I arrived the lights were on, so I knew Erik was around. The door to his office was open and I went in, just to say that I would be there for the rest of the afternoon. Erik was on the floor behind his desk, with blood all over him. I called nine one one on his phone, and then I saw his suicide note on the desk. Erik wasn't breathing, and I was sure he was dead. While I waited for the ambulance to arrive, I went into my office and read his note. The police were angry with me for having moved it, but at the time I just wanted to understand what had happened."

"Of course," said Elizabeth. "I'm sure I would've felt the same way."

"It was all terrible. Erik's note was pitiful. It tried to explain how he got caught up in the S and L scene of the last few years. He needed money and, because he was well known as a developer, he found it was easy to borrow large amounts under his own, not the partnership's, name. Even for development projects that only existed on paper. When payments for that first loan came due, he simply borrowed more from another S and L. He never started a building project, but just kept borrowing. Like you hear about on *60 Minutes,* you see. The cycle continued until last quarter when the market took a downturn and all the banks had to pull back. He found he couldn't get any more loans to pay off the previous ones, and he slipped toward default. Last week he learned that the feds were starting to investigate him. With John dead, there was no one to help him here at work. When I look back at these last few weeks, I can see things I didn't notice at the time that should've made me think about suicide. I suppose he was just holding on through the memorial service. Then he felt everything was over. He must have gone straight from your Meetinghouse to our office. I'm sorry I didn't do the same."

Elizabeth extended her condolences to Muriel for this, the second death so near to her.

"It's difficult to adjust to everything," responded Muriel, "and I will miss them both, especially John."

"Was Erik's note handwritten?" asked Elizabeth.

"Oh, yes," said Muriel. "That's what made it clear to the police I wasn't involved, I think. It was a long, handwritten note, full of Erik's ramblings."

"Did it say anything about John or his death?"

"It said he was sorry that John's name might be associated with his financial problems. His note made it clear he had acted as an individual, not for the partnership, on the S and L loans."

Elizabeth thanked Muriel for telling her this sad story and wished her the best.

Sunday evening Elizabeth went to bed early. Clerking the Business Meeting, and the news about Erik, had tired her greatly. Her arthritic pain was not bad at all, but she felt deeply worn out by the stress of the recent days. With gratitude she said her evening prayers and prepared for bed. Just before retiring, she took a dose of her new blood pressure medicine and soon fell asleep.

But at 1 A.M. Elizabeth awoke, shaking and sweating. She felt confused and wondered if she had a fever. After throwing off the covers and lying still for a few minutes, she felt better.

I must've had a bad dream, she thought. She recalled that in the months immediately after her husband's death, nightmares had often awakened her in the early hours of the morning.

Elizabeth pulled the sheet and blanket back over her again and drifted into a light sleep. She watched a confused scene in the Meetinghouse. People were sitting silently in worship while the body of John Hoffman lay on one of the front benches. She knew this was improper and rose to speak about it. Other Quakers began to rise to their feet, and Elizabeth sat down again to hear what others had to say. One by one all the Friends present said, "I'm not guilty. It was someone else." In the end, everyone present said this, in exactly the same tone and manner. Tim Schouweiler, who was not there, came into Elizabeth's mind. "No," she said emphatically, "that can't be. Someone here must be lying." For a moment the dream became hazy as Elizabeth rolled over in bed.

Suddenly she was at the front door of John's house and he was standing beside her. She knew that something was strange. The house looked just the same as always, but John was chalk-white. He unlocked the door and held it open for her. She hesitated and said, "John, you're dead now."

John did not reply but stepped through the doorway. He continued to hold the door open and beckoned for Elizabeth to follow. Again she hesitated. "Your nephew owns this place now, John. I don't think it's right for me to go inside."

John shook his head and smiled at her. He again beckoned for her to follow him and then reached out and gently took hold of her wrist. He did not pull her through the doorway, but waited for her to make up her mind. Elizabeth said, "I don't feel right about this. . . ." John continued to smile at her, and Elizabeth stepped into his house.

As she entered, John Hoffman vanished. Elizabeth found herself in his front entrance quite alone. The front door had been closed after her. She was under the impression that she must search for something, for John's presence somewhere in the house. She began to search the living room carefully.

Again, Elizabeth awoke. She was neither sweating nor shaking this time. The dream was strong and clear in her mind. Elizabeth was not superstitious about dreams, but the conviction that she should go to John's house was deep. Her head felt good. The pain and heaviness within her skull were entirely gone. If she were to be open to God's leading, surely she must pay attention to such strong and clear feelings as she now had. As she lay in the darkness, she resolved to go to John's house in the morning.

Rain was striking the roof when Elizabeth awoke at 7:00 A.M. Her shoulder joints ached in sympathy with the rain, but her hands were not as painful as usual in such weather. She looked through her window at the dark and wet scene outside. Concord Avenue was full of traffic splashing through the water in the street. Still fatigued, she dressed slowly. She brewed herself strong tea, ate some toast, and took her morning dose of arthritis and blood pressure pills. Putting on her wool-lined raincoat and taking her biggest umbrella, Elizabeth armed herself against the elements. Leaving her house, she walked up Concord Avenue toward Huron and Royal. Rain had been falling steadily for some time and the gutters of Cambridge were filled. Passing cars, driving at speeds which Elizabeth considered reckless, sprayed water onto the passing pedestrians. There was nothing that people on foot could do to protect themselves.

Wetter than she liked to be, Elizabeth turned up Royal Avenue. She passed Jane Thompson's house and then paused for a moment at the head of the sidewalk leading to the door of John Hoffman's place. Part of Elizabeth's mind knew that what she was doing was wrong. She felt like a thief. On the other hand, what she had experienced during the night had been clear. She had not known that being clerk would bring such moral dilemmas. But she needed to resolve the problems surrounding John's death before further harm came to Tim Schouweiler or any other innocent man. She felt called about this visit. She walked up to the front door, not looking to her right or left, took out her duplicate key, and let herself in.

Elizabeth closed the door behind her and then regretted it. The weather was so dark, the rain so heavy, that in the front hall of the house she could hardly see a thing. In a moment, however, she had found the light switch and proceeded through the first floor of the house turning on more lights than were strictly necessary.

Elizabeth took off her coat and laid it, still dripping, across a chair near the back door. She left her umbrella beside it. Wanting to keep the floor dry, she paused to put down several old newspapers under the chair.

Since she was near the back hallway where John stored his journals, she decided to begin her search there. She stooped down to better see the long row of volumes. She took out the oldest of the journals and, sitting down on a stool next to the back door, began to read. She skimmed the entries, moving gradually through the 1960s. The books followed the same basic pattern as the 1990 volume she had previously read. The first dozen pages dealt only with gardening questions and clippings about roses. There followed a traditional Quaker journal with daily entries. John had recorded his thoughts about Meeting and spiritual life only briefly during this period. His entries concerning business were longer and seemed an unreflective record of a rising real estate developer.

Elizabeth skipped forward to 1980 and began to read more slowly and thoroughly. John had continued to record his business dealings, and the business continued to prosper. However, the entries concerning religious work and spiritual life were now much longer and more detailed. He repeatedly reported his efforts to spend more time in prayer. And every three or four months Elizabeth found an entry relating mystical experiences. He attempted to describe them by saying he was filled with an inner fire, reminding one of Pascal's record of an experience put down in his *Pensées*. Elizabeth had known such experiences frequently in childhood and still was given them on occasion.

John had been part of a small prayer group, a "Village Meeting," from 1981 to 1984, and there were detailed notes about his prayers in these Meetings. At this time John began a systematic study of the Bible, and the summaries of his readings and Village Meeting discussions were impressive evidence of how much he cared about the Christian life. A few entries were well organized and read almost like homilies, but most were more simple recordings of ideas not fully developed. Still, his writings on biblical themes or village life were impressive. Elizabeth felt guilt that her own life was comparatively weak. Her journal entries seldom reached the length that John's routinely did, and he clearly wrote some of them in the grip of powerful spiritual experiences.

By the late 1980s, John's journal barely mentioned his work. From notations he made it was clear he felt financially secure. Once he asked himself why he didn't retire right away.

In 1989 several entries were devoted to the subject of Erik Swensen, who had hardly been mentioned earlier. The entries made it clear that John was concerned about Erik personally and was alarmed at some of the transactions his partner was making. "Little of his operating money is tapped from partnership funds," John had written. "I'm not sure where he's getting the capital for his sideline transactions, but as long as it doesn't involve partnership money I'm reluctant to say anything—unless he asks for help. We all must find our own paths in this world. I know I cannot impose my ideas on Erik. Perhaps I will be able to bail him out, if the situation is not too bad—hard to know how deep in he is under these new S & L practices."

Elizabeth continued to read through the 1989 journal and then looked for 1990, the volume she had taken to her house and then returned. With a start she realized that the 1989 volume had been the last in the row. The 1990 journal was gone.

9

In all the best generations of Quakerism, the ideal aim and the controlling expectation of the wiser members have been to live the simple life. It is, of course, a vague and indefinable term . . . It begins inside with the quality of the soul. It is first and foremost the quality of sincerity, which is the opposite of duplicity or sham . . . Unclouded honesty at the heart and centre of the man is the true basis of simplicity . . .

Rufus Jones, 1927

Elizabeth left John Hoffman's house in a determined frame of mind. The rain splattered all around her and she was soaked again, but she hardly noticed. She was aware of her arthritis pain, but only as an abstraction. She walked quickly home and hung up her dripping coat in the hall on the way to the kitchen. She called Bill at his work and sternly explained that she needed to speak to him.

Bill sighed. He seemed to resent being interrupted at his office as he asked Elizabeth what was on her mind.

"Our Business Meeting yesterday makes it clear that Friends may have difficulty accepting John's bequest," replied the Clerk. "That seems reasonable to me, because of the circumstances of his death. And I am concerned that he intended the money to go to several different groups he had talked to me about, not to us. The groups included the soup kitchen in Harvard Square and the Friends Service Committee."

Elizabeth paused. She expected Bill to say something, but he was silent.

"I know John was in the habit of keeping a detailed journal. He and I used to talk about journal writing. I'm afraid my own efforts in that direction have been sporadic, but I think John was quite faithful to his journal. Would you be so kind as to look in his house for his journals or lend me your key again and I'll go?"

Bill answered with hostility. "And what do you think his journals could help you with?"

"It's likely," replied Elizabeth in a calm voice, "that they'd show his thinking this year about his finances. What he said in Meeting for Worship the day before his death made it clear he was in some transition. I'm sure his journal would show something about what his wishes were just before he died. The Meeting shouldn't accept a large sum of money from his estate if he intended it to go elsewhere.''

"Where the money goes is, first of all, a legal question. By law, it's my uncle's will that matters. The will you heard read by Bradford Smith is the only will that my uncle had. I know my uncle used to keep a detailed journal, but he told me this past New Year's he was giving it up. There would be no journal for this year, 1990, so I don't see the point in your searching for something that doesn't exist."

Elizabeth considered. She had not been prepared for open falsehood from a fellow Quaker. As she looked out her back window at the juncos feeding, she condemned herself mentally for her naïveté. For the moment, she did not want to go further with Bill.

"I see," she replied. "Well, in that case, perhaps I'd better talk to those who knew John best and see if anyone knows what he was intending."

This stopped Bill for a moment. Then he said, "If anyone knew anything definite I'm sure he would have spoken up yesterday at the Business Meeting. Face it, we only have Uncle John's will to go on. That document is legally valid and it's clear."

Elizabeth demurred. She thanked Bill for his time, apologized for interrupting him at work, and hung up. She needed to pause and pray and consider her next move. Sparkle, who had watched the telephone conversation from a kitchen chair, looked intently at her mistress and, for a moment, Elizabeth thought the cat was on the verge of speech.

I must be awfully distressed to imagine such a thing, she thought as she sat down. Sparkle, without apology, slipped off to the basement.

Throughout the afternoon she struggled with her thoughts, truly in a quandary. As the evening began, she was still trying to make a decision about what she must do. She realized that she was in danger of going far astray from Quaker practice. She could no longer continue on her path of half truths and deceit. Sitting at her kitchen table, awash with feelings of confusion and fear for Bill, she prayed for help. She realized she was in need of a Clearness Committee, for she could not find her way alone any longer.

Although the Meeting had a formal mechanism for nominating Friends to compose such a committee, Elizabeth realized she did not have time to wait. She called Patience Silverstone and explained that she was in need of help and advice. She asked Patience if she would be willing to be a one-person Clearness Committee and meet with Elizabeth that very evening. Patience, surprised by the question, asked what the problem was.

"I'm not sure how to answer that over the phone," replied Elizabeth, "but it concerns both John Hoffman's murder and some actions I've taken. I want to know who is responsible for his death."

"I see," said Patience slowly. "I didn't know that any Friends were actively aiding the police."

"No, it's not the police I'm trying to help. They are busy with other things. For quite a while, they were sure that one of our homeless attenders, the man named Tim, was guilty. I've showed that wasn't true. I'm afraid that one of our members is guilty. In fact, I'm now sure that a Friend is lying in connection with John's money. The money may well be connected with his death."

Patience paused before replying. She had known Elizabeth for half a century and knew she was a careful Friend who would not speak without cause.

"If thee feels the need of the Clearness process, Ministry and Council will nominate Friends to help thee."

"Yes," answered Elizabeth, "I realize that. But in this case I feel pressured for time. I'm afraid that one of our members has been destroying evidence related to John's death. I need Clearness now!"

Patience realized that a long talk was needed. That had best be done in person.

"Come to my house, right now, and we can talk about everything."

Elizabeth agreed and said good-bye. She felt a bit of relief, simply from having taken action.

Patience lived in a small house, just two blocks from the Meetinghouse. Beyond Longfellow Park there was a neighborhood of narrow, mostly dead-end streets, which had now become upscale. Patience had been living in her little house since the 1940s. She had little respect for many of her neighbors and their materialistic life-style. But the house was hers, and it was so close to the Meetinghouse, she had never had the strength to leave it. Some of her friends were now beginning to advise Patience to move to some kind of retirement community. Her eighty-fifth birthday had reminded everyone that she would not be active and alert forever. But since she still had her strength, she was resisting these suggestions. As Elizabeth walked down Concord Avenue and through Longfellow Park, she was glad that Patience lived so close.

The elderly Quaker let Elizabeth in through the front door and recommended they sit in the kitchen. Leading Elizabeth to the small, orderly kitchen, she explained, "It's warmer here than in the living room, Friend."

Both women sat down, and Elizabeth tried to compose her thoughts.

"Start at the beginning. We have all evening," said Patience.

"Thank you," replied Elizabeth. She told Patience the

whole truth, omitting none of her thoughts and actions. To her, the story seemed to go on for a long time, but as she reached the end she knew her decision had been the right one. She had borne this burden alone for too long.

Patience listened with the respect of one old Quaker for another. When Elizabeth had finished summarizing her most recent conversation with Bill and her decision to call Patience and ask for help in finding Clearness, the elder of the two asked for silence. Two friends sat in the quiet of the kitchen, trying to listen for God's voice.

For Elizabeth, the relief of having spoken was great, and she prayed with a grateful heart for further guidance. She felt the silence of the room wash over her and had the sensation of diving into water, delightfully warm and pure. When she resurfaced and opened her eyes, she saw that Patience was still in prayer. Quietly, Elizabeth waited.

After a time, Patience raised her head, opened her eyes, and smiled at Elizabeth.

"Friend, I'm glad thee came. Hast thee found anything here?"

"Yes, it seems clear to me now I must confront Bill with what I know about the journal and its disappearance."

"That feels right to me," replied Patience. "No more time should pass without honesty. If William is guilty, that's something he needs to face. And the Meeting must face it, too. That won't be easy, especially for those of us who have known and respected him for so long."

"I think I should approach Bill right away. There's nothing to be gained by delay. Would you be willing to be with me when I talk to Bill?"

"Yes," answered Patience. "Let's call him now. It's rather late in the day for someone my age to make a trip, so perhaps thee might invite him to come here."

Bill was at home. He was startled by the invitation. He rather ungraciously agreed to come to Patience's house.

As they waited for Bill's arrival, Patience brought out crackers and cheese. It was clear that a proper supper might not be possible for anyone this evening, and some nourishment was necessary to keep minds functioning. As she ate a cracker, Elizabeth thanked her friend for once again being such a help in her time of need.

"When Michael died," she said, "I remember that you were always present for me. And tonight you are a tremendous help once again."

"This situation is certainly an unusual one for a Clerk to handle," said Patience. "Now that I think of it, I can see we have been avoiding the real problem of John's death. If anyone in Meeting is connected with his death, or even with removing evidence about the murder, clearly we have a responsibility to respond to that. I'm afraid our group hasn't been thinking about the actual murder. It's easier to deny that kind of thing than to live with it. I'm not saying I feel comfortable with all our Clerk's actions, Friend, but using them as a beginning we should all be able to think about this situation more clearly. We can't allow this uncertainty to continue in our midst. Thee hast done us some good, Clerk. But use different methods next time."

Elizabeth accepted what she felt was just criticism and also accepted what she hoped was just praise. She had finished the food, and she leaned back in her chair. Patience cleared away the few dishes. Just as she was finishing, the doorbell rang.

Patience opened the door to Bill and took his coat. He was moving stiffly. He saw Elizabeth through the kitchen door and briefly nodded to her.

"Come into the kitchen, William," said Patience. "We're sitting here because it's the warmest room."

Bill came in and sat in the chair nearest the door. Looking from Patience to Elizabeth, he said rather crossly, "I'm here."

"And thank you for coming. It's a difficult evening for us all, I'm sure. We need to talk, Bill, and talk better than we did earlier today. I was in your uncle's house this morning."

"How could you have been there?"

"I have a key, as it happens."

"Perhaps thee should start at the beginning, Friend," said Patience.

"Yes, you're right," responded Elizabeth. She paused to collect her thoughts. "When I got the news that John was dead, I assumed it was a natural death."

"As we all did," said Bill.

Elizabeth looked at him. She could not understand what was in Bill's mind, however, so she continued. "When I knew that his death was a murder, I hoped that the matter had nothing to do with the Meeting."

Again Bill interrupted her. "Right. It looks like the murder was done by Tim, yes? That's really not a Meeting concern."

"It certainly is, Friend," put in Patience. "I'm afraid I don't know Tim. I've never really spoken to him. But he has been one of our attenders for several years, hasn't he? He's part of the Meeting. Some members hardly darken our doors, after all."

"A half-crazy homeless man may come to Meeting, he may even come regularly," said Bill, "but that hardly makes him a Friend. Did I come here to discuss membership with you?" asked Bill with exasperation in his voice.

"Bill, you're not speaking the truth, and that's why we are all here." Elizabeth looked directly at him as she said, "The murder is a Meeting concern. And, furthermore, Tim is guilty of nothing. He can establish where he was on the afternoon of your uncle's death. I checked with the Salvation Army people. He spent the afternoon there asleep in their clothing room."

"Fine," answered Bill. "But even if you accept his story, I don't see what this really has to do with me."

"You are connected to this crime in some way," responded Elizabeth. Her voice grew harder as she said, "I'm sure of that now."

Bill looked at her intently. His eyes narrowed and he said, "You had better explain what you mean."

"Your uncle had just finished going through a long spiritual journey. We have two pieces of evidence for that. Adam Chrisler knew about that journey. He knew as much as a private person like your uncle would allow. And secondly, your uncle's journals are detailed and complete, as you know. In the volume for this year, he recorded one of the results of his journey. He was going to give away all his wealth, and do so by New Year's. He asked you, as his lawyer, to draw up whatever papers were necessary. You were still his lawyer, weren't you? The pending judgeship or no, your uncle turned to you to take care of these legal tasks for him. The journal is clear on those points, Bill."

"That's what you were getting at on the phone, then," responded Bill, his shoulders now sagging. He put his elbows on the table and his head in his hands. "And you've been to my uncle's house today?"

"That's right. I felt called to go back there again. I'm sorry, Bill, but I copied the key you lent me earlier. It was wrong to do so, as Patience surely agrees, and I knew it was dishonest. I confess both to doing it and to knowing it to be wrong. Today I felt led back to John's house. I carefully read his journals from past years. The journal for this year, as you must know, is gone. I had read it when I first visited the house.

"I lied to you, and on more than one occasion. But, Friend, you have been lying, too. You said that your uncle stopped keeping his journal. Actually, you've taken it and probably destroyed it. It's the only hard evidence that shows you were about to lose your inheritance."

Patience said in her gentle voice, "It seems clear thee hast been destroying evidence. That will be known to the Meeting when all this comes out. Thee, our past Clerk of the Finance Committee, member of Ministry and Counsel. It's difficult to accept, and I for one have been reluctant to think about any of this. Can't thee be honest with us now?"

"All right! I'll tell you what happened!" answered Bill. His face, which he had removed from his hands, was red with emotion. "It's true I've lied. My uncle had some hare-brained ideas about giving away all his money. He talked to me on Sunday, the day before he died, at Meeting. He gave me a list of pinko and Catholic organizations he wanted it all to go to. He wanted me to figure what taxes would be owed by the end of the year and then disburse everything he had. I told him I thought it irresponsible and thoughtless! He would have nothing to live on. He only laughed and said he was 'free' of all that. I knew I'd not only lose my inheritance, I'd end up supporting him. And this is not the time for me to take on a dependent! My income will be going down when I become a judge. I want to be on the bench, it's been a long-term goal of mine. Since becoming a partner, I've thought of it and been working toward it with the governor's office. But compared to my private practice, it's not a well-paying job.

"I told my uncle what a fool he was for even considering such a thing. He put the papers in my suit-coat pocket and said I should call him when I had the taxes worked out. I shouted at him for a while. We were standing in Longfellow Park, quite a way from the Meetinghouse, and I didn't think any Friends could hear us."

"Nobody did, I think, except my niece, and she doesn't know either of you, so she didn't pay attention to the scene," responded Elizabeth. She waited a moment and then added, "Did you go home?"

"Yes," said Bill. "Straight from that argument I went home. At home I thought it all over and I was more convinced than ever that the scheme was mad. It wasn't the calling of God my uncle was hearing, it was the need to make his old age dramatic."

"A dramatic old age and the calling of God needn't be incompatible, Friend," said Patience.

"No. But it was crazy all the same. I could see I was losing my family's inheritance. It was all going to go to Central America and soup kitchens. And I, the only person left in the family, would have to support my uncle till the day he died."

"That was not long, as it turned out," said Elizabeth.

"Don't accuse me of murder!" snarled Bill. "Don't you see, that's what I've been so afraid of, and that's what has led me to do such stupid things. I didn't kill my uncle! The thought is appalling! Surely you can believe that!"

"What happened to the journal?" asked Elizabeth.

"After I lent you the key I thought of his journal and realized I had been a real fool. If he had recorded his thoughts about money, you can see that I might be a suspect. I went to his house the night you returned the key to me. I found the journals and decided only the last one was really problematic. The others I left. Apart from this year's journal, all there was was what Uncle John had said in Meeting for Worship the day before he died. And that was rather vague. I decided to say that yes, my uncle had been rethinking his money situation and he talked to me about it in a general way, but nothing definite was in his mind."

"What happened to the journal?" repeated Elizabeth.

"I have it," answered Bill. "Maybe I could be disbarred for this. Certainly I could lose my chance at the bench. I ask you two to remember how much that means to me! But I admit I have the journal. The police haven't been looking for it. I haven't destroyed any evidence. So I don't think I could actually be disbarred. But if I give the journal to Burnham now, please don't tell everything you know to the Meeting. I couldn't bear that, and what Meeting knows might somehow make it to the bar. It only takes a little hint of wrongdoing for the statehouse to throw out an appointment."

Bill stopped to catch his breath. Elizabeth said to him quietly, "What Patience and I know need not be known by everyone. But, Bill, you must see that we can't just accept what you are saying now, given that you have been lying to us. Tell the truth and we all can face it together. Where did you go after you left work? Directly to The Station? And where did you go when you left that bar?"

Bill's face became set and hard. He looked directly at Elizabeth and said, "I don't have to tell you that. What right do you have to elder me? The hypocrisy in Meeting is enormous!"

Saying that, he got up, walked to the front door, got his coat, and left. Patience and Elizabeth made no move to stop him.

10

So it is possible for Friends to sympathize with the sincerity of all religious seekers. In this spirit they discover with Peter, after his vision, "Of truth I perceive that God is no respecter of persons; but in every nation he that feareth him, and worketh righteousness, is accepted with him."

Mary Blackmar, early-twentieth-century American Quaker

Tim Schouweiler sat on his bunk, smoking one of the cigarettes given to him by Adam. Tim was surprised that Adam had come to visit. He knew Adam from Quaker Meeting, of course, but only in passing. It seemed strange to Tim that Adam and the old lady from the Meeting had taken such an interest in him once the police picked him up. Not many Quakers had had a kind word to say to Tim when he was on the streets, after all.

Tim was a bit puzzled by Quakers, but he no longer worried about them. In fact, he felt little interest even in himself. He was lost these days, not in thought, but in a kind of detached despondency. Nothing in life had looked hopeful to Tim for a long time, but jail had made everything even more dreary. He was hardly sleeping at night, even here in the warmth of the jail, and he ate little of what they brought him. At present, he was sitting in a foggy state of mind and smoking.

A guard stopped at his cell and fumbled with keys for a moment, then opened the door. Tim sat still, hoping the man would go away.

"Schouweiler!" said the guard. "Good news! You're outta here. The guy at the end of the hall will sign you out and give you your personal stuff back."

Tim looked blankly at the guard. He forced himself to concentrate on what the man had said. The general meaning of it began to sink in, and Tim ground out his cigarette.

"They're letting me out?" he asked quietly.

"Yup, that's what I said. The charges against you've been dropped. Hurry up, will ya? Get your clothes together and come with me."

Tim's clothes consisted of a spare coverall from the jail supplies and an extra pair of socks. He picked up both and put them under his arm, then pocketed the cigarettes and matches.

"You want yer book?" asked the guard, indicating a murder mystery in Tim's cell.

Tim shook his head. "What's the weather like?" he asked.

"It was cold when I come to work, and it's raining hard. Sorry about that, but out you go."

The two men walked down the corridor, Tim one step behind the guard. He was given back a few pocket items he had had with him and the sweater and pants he had on when he was arrested. As he changed clothes, he asked what day of the week it was. The guards told him it was Monday.

Tim emerged on the streets of Central Square. He immediately began to shiver in the cold rain. He stood still for quite a while in the middle of the sidewalk, wondering where he might go to survive the day. Passersby hurried around him, their hats and umbrellas protecting them from the worst of the weather. No one looked at Tim. The homeless man, now wet to the skin, asked one of them for the time. It was noon. Tim thought about his options for lunch, and after a minute he started to walk toward the Salvation Army building.

As the day passed, Tim began to find the rhythm of street life once again. He did not feel as dejected as he had in jail. His mind cleared as the day progressed.

The rain stopped in the afternoon, and when it did Tim decided to try his luck panhandling in Harvard Square. Yuppies did not give the homeless a penny when it was raining because they did not want to be slowed down in any way when the weather was bad. But after a rainstorm, as the sky cleared, the pace of yuppies on the sidewalk slowed and they became more generous to the indigent. That, at least, was Tim's general experience. And Harvard Square gave him a high concentration of yuppies. He stood outside the

Harvard Cooperative bookstore, called "the Coop" by Cambridge residents, who rhymed the name with "loop." He tried his luck with the upscale crowd. By the time he had collected two dollars, the sun was out. He bought half a sandwich at Au Bon Pain, leaving him fourteen cents. He took his food two blocks to Cambridge Common and ate on a park bench. He preferred the Common to eating in the presence of the well-to-do in Harvard Square.

As he sat in the Common, looking at Christ Church, his mind drifted back to the day the police had taken him in. He remembered clearly the Elliot woman visiting him at the soup kitchen meal. From there he thought back to the last Sunday John Hoffman had been alive. It had been a difficult morning for Tim. He remembered his pain and confusion. But he also recalled the man in a terrific argument with a younger man in Longfellow Park between the morning meeting and the afternoon one. Tim thought the younger man was also a Hoffman, although he could not remember his first name. He could still hear what the younger Quaker had been shouting at John, though, and it was impressive what quiet Quakers could scream at each other when money was concerned. Perhaps, thought Tim, he would look up Elizabeth and tell her what had happened and what he had heard.

Elizabeth had just come in from refilling the bird feeder in her backyard when the telephone rang. It was Bill on the line and he began with an apology.

"I'm deeply sorry about the way I treated you and Patience last night. All I can say is that the stress I have felt in the last couple of weeks is making me a stranger even to myself. But that's no excuse for refusing to talk to you two, and no excuse for walking out on Friends without a word of good-bye."

"Thank you for saying that," responded Elizabeth. "I'm sure Patience and I recognize what deep stress can do, and our feelings were not hurt last night. But the problem of needing to understand this situation continues."

"Yes. I've thought about it all night and I can see that. I've resented your poking your nose into this, Elizabeth, but now I can see that you wouldn't be much of a Friend if you didn't. I want now to tell you where I was late in the afternoon on that Monday. I hope you will double-check my story so that you can be sure of what I'm saying. It's the truth, but it's a truth I would be glad if the rest of the Meeting, even Patience, need not know about.

"I went to The Station after I left work, just as I told you. I saw Tom Redburn there and spoke to him for a minute. A friend of mine came to the bar just then and, as often in the past, I left with him and went to his house. It's in Cambridge, near Davis Square. We tried to take the subway, but it wasn't running, and so we took the number thirty-three bus that runs up Massachusetts Avenue. I was with my friend until six o'clock. I left his place just as *MacNeil-Lehrer* was coming on the TV.

"The reason I didn't tell you this is that my friend is not out of the closet. He works at Harvard in a highly visible job and he wouldn't want exposure, I'm sure."

"I see," said Elizabeth, "but what would this friend of yours wish if he knew the seriousness of the situation?"

"I hope he will do the right thing when it's clear to him how important this is. He doesn't know about the murder, I'm sure, it's not as if a murder is big news in this city. In fact he left town for meetings in Berkeley the day after I was at his house, so he wouldn't have seen anything in the *Globe.* He's back in town now; he called me on Saturday. We couldn't get together, and at that time I saw no reason to bring this subject up."

Elizabeth waited. After a moment of hesitation, Bill continued. "I'm still hopeful that my friend will face up to the police and tell them where I was during those hours. But I must admit I'm a little unsure about him, because he so much fears exposure. We all do, I guess, but he has it worse than most. Before I tell the police all this, I hoped you might speak to him yourself. He can confirm what I've said, and I think he'll do so if you ask. At this point, I care more about what my Meeting and Clerk think than I do about the police and the Bar Association and even the Senate. His name is James Reynolds. He's on the senior faculty of the law school at Harvard. He was a young professor when I was a student there; that's how we met."

Elizabeth considered. Bill waited for her reply. It was brief when it came. "I'll speak to Professor Reynolds today," she said. "Perhaps we can all have some peace soon."

Immediately after hanging up, Elizabeth called the law school and ascertained from a secretary that James Reynolds was in his office this morning. Elizabeth gave her name and asked to speak to him. The secretary asked what her business was. Elizabeth said she was the Clerk of Cambridge's Quaker Meeting and the matter she wished to discuss was personal. The secretary asked her to hold the line and when she came back on she said that Professor Reynolds would be happy to deal with her concern, if that were appropriate, and that she should put it in writing and send it to his office. Elizabeth asked where the office was, and once she understood that, she explained to the secretary that she would come over directly to Harvard and speak to the professor in person.

Elizabeth walked down Concord Avenue with a purposeful stride. She cut across the common and stepped onto Harvard property. The law school was next to Massachusetts Avenue, and she reached it quickly. The main building of the law school was a long, stone structure covered with ivy. It faced a little yard of its own. When Elizabeth's children were young she had occasionally walked them to this part of the grounds. She had clear memories of Andrew chasing his brother around the elms and oaks. As she saw the law school yard again she felt a pang for the past.

Professor Reynolds's office was easy to find. She entered. A secretary was typing but stopped immediately. In a stern voice she said, "You must be Mrs. Elliot. You have to understand that we do business here in an orderly way and the senior faculty are busy men. You can state your problem here on this pad and I'll personally make sure that Professor Reynolds looks at it today. If it's appropriate, I'll call you tomorrow so you can set up an appointment to see him."

"I understand that's your normal procedure for people you don't know," answered Elizabeth.

"And for people who won't state their business," said the secretary sharply.

"But in this case a different procedure is needed. I can't state my business to you, only to Mr. Reynolds, to whom you wouldn't put me through on the telephone. I can wait here, however, until he is able to see me. My business will only take five minutes of his time."

"I can't let you force yourself into his schedule, Mrs. Elliot," replied the secretary. "It sets a terrible precedent."

"Not many old Quaker ladies are going to force themselves into his day, I assure you. You can let me state my business to him without the collapse of normal business at the law school." Saying this, Elizabeth drew up a chair next to the inner door of the office. She reasoned that it must lead to Mr. Reynolds, or at least in his direction. The only other door was the one she had come in from the hall.

The secretary was now glaring at her. "We have work to do here. We cannot have people off the street demanding space in our office."

"I'll be happy to wait until Mr. Reynolds can see me," answered Elizabeth in a gentle tone. "And then, I assure you, I will be happy to leave."

"I'll call security unless you behave more reasonably," said the secretary.

"Kirsten," said a tall man in tweeds, opening the inner door, "I need this typed before lunch."

Elizabeth was on her feet and held out her hand. Automatically the man took it in a brief shake, looking puzzled.

"I'm Elizabeth Elliot, I'm here on personal business and I won't take more than two minutes of your time, but I must speak to you today."

James Reynolds looked peeved. He gave Kirsten a look but motioned Elizabeth into his office.

"Since you're so insistent, I'll give you two minutes, but it won't be more than that. I have a meeting with the dean at eleven and I won't be late."

Elizabeth did not bother to sit down. She took this man at his word and hoped he would take her at hers. She unbuttoned her coat and said, "I've come here to save a friend of yours from needless suspicion and distrust. A man named John Hoffman was murdered here in Cambridge on Columbus Day. Were you aware of that?"

"No," said the distinguished professor. He looked at her thoughtfully and sat down in his chair.

"He was the uncle of William Hoffman. Both Hoffmans have been members of Quaker Meeting here for many years. I'm Clerk of that Meeting, which is a little bit like being a chairman.

"Bill is to inherit a substantial amount of money because of his uncle's death. The murder took place between four and six P.M. on Columbus Day. Until now, police attention has focused on a homeless man from our Meeting who knew John well. But evidence has made it clear that he could not have killed John Hoffman."

Elizabeth paused for just a moment to make sure that the professor was with her. He was a sharp man and had kept up with this briefing. He nodded his head for her to continue.

"Bill Hoffman will now be the leading suspect for the police. And his position in the Quaker community is becoming more than awkward. He tells me he was with you at your house for the time in question on the afternoon of Columbus Day. He has tried to shield you from this, but the time has come for an honest account of what happened that day. Innocent people suffer otherwise.

"Will you at least tell me where you were that afternoon? That will help Bill keep his position as a Quaker. And will you tell the police as well?"

Professor James Reynolds considered only briefly.

"Yes," he responded. "Clearly this is a time to set aside personal interests. I met Bill on Columbus Day in Central Square, at a place called The Station. We went to my house in north Cambridge. We went by bus, actually, because the Red Line was down. He was with me until the evening."

"Can you say when he left, exactly?" asked Elizabeth.

"Not really," answered the professor. "It was quite dark. I remember turning on the outside light when he left. So it must have been about six, or a bit after. He didn't stay to watch the news, I remember that, because *MacNeil-*

Lehrer had a special interview with one of his classmates here which I thought he would have enjoyed. One doesn't know in advance who they will put on on a given night."

Elizabeth relaxed. Her main goal in speaking to this man had been achieved. She asked, "Will you make this same statement to the police?"

"Of course." There was finality in his voice.

"The man there to speak to is Detective Burnham," said Elizabeth. "He is in the homicide department."

James Reynolds stood up and held the door open for her to leave. Kirsten was busy typing and kept her eyes on her work as Elizabeth walked out into the hallway. She buttoned her coat and went directly home. The Clerk had never felt so old.

The telephone awakened Elizabeth from her postlunch nap. She answered with a bit of irritation. It was Jane Thompson on the line. Jane had been reading the sensation-loving *Boston Herald* about the unfolding S and L crisis. There she had seen mention of Erik Swensen's death.

"Wasn't that John's business partner?" she asked.

"Yes," answered Elizabeth, a bit of her weariness showing through in her voice, "I'm afraid it was. He was at our Meeting for John last Saturday and then went to his office. He killed himself there."

"Really!" said Jane. "That makes things different, doesn't it?"

Elizabeth asked what she meant.

"But don't you see? Everybody has been trying to find out who killed John, if it wasn't that dirty homeless man in Meeting, which I still think it was, even if you don't. But maybe we've been thinking about this wrong. John was killed, and now his business partner, too. That seems to point to someone at work, doesn't it?"

"The police don't think there was any foul play involved in Erik's death," answered Elizabeth. "He had run out of luck, it seems, in some fraudulent games he was playing with the banks. The federal people had begun an investigation of him and he faced financial ruin."

"Who found him?"

"The secretary in the partnership, a woman I know a little, is the one who found the body. Don't suspect her, Jane, she was in Lexington the afternoon that John was killed and she didn't kill Erik Swensen. The suicide note he left was handwritten by him, and the police are satisfied his death was his own doing."

"But then who could have killed our John? Don't tell me it was a Friend!"

"God willing," replied Elizabeth, whose patience with that thought had ended long ago, "we'll know more about that soon." She wished Jane a good afternoon and hung up before she could speak.

Elizabeth baked a quick bread, more to fill up the afternoon with some positive activity than because sweet bread was needed. Grating the peel of two oranges and with a small bag of frozen cranberries, she put together three little loaves of bread appropriate to the season. While they were in the oven, Sparkle silently appeared in the kitchen, and Elizabeth fed the cat liberally.

"Friends can do no wrong, Sparkle. That's what too many Quakers will tell you. There's no need for repentance when there's no transgression, you see."

Sparkle, never a committed student of theology, was happy to listen and eat at the same time.

"Maybe we could use the confessional in the Society of Friends. Manned by the janitor of each Meeting, perhaps. Just the idea would shake up a lot of Quakers. We need to look at ourselves, Friend. Error is not such a great sin as denial.''

Elizabeth left off lecturing the cat to take the quick bread out of the oven. It looked like a successful batch. Slightly cheered, she went upstairs to soak her arthritic bones in a hot bath.

Later the same afternoon Elizabeth received a call from Bill. He had been to see Burnham and given him a new statement about the events of the Columbus Day weekend. He had also given Burnham his uncle's journal. The detective had accepted the journal and Bill's new version of events without much comment. He lectured Bill on obstructing justice, but since he had come in voluntarily to repair the damage he had done, Burnham was inclined to let the matter rest. This Bill viewed as a lifesaver, for his actions might merit disbarment if the police chose to make an issue of them and they came to the attention of the Massachusetts Bar Association, the people involved in reviewing his appointment to the judicial branch of the Commonwealth's government. James Reynolds had called Bill and assured him he had already written out a statement for the police about the afternoon in question.

Elizabeth expressed her gladness that Bill had come forward with the whole story and congratulated him on the courage required to do so.

"It's admirable, Friend, that you came forward while you thought it could do you real professional harm. Not many of us could manage that.''

"Well,'' said Bill, "it's good to be relieved of the burdens of secrecy. The most wretched way of living is with constant deceit.''

Elizabeth agreed, and they said good-bye. When she hung up the telephone, she offered a joyful prayer of thanksgiving. One of her prayers had been fully answered.

. . .

The specially called Business Meeting the following evening was well attended. Looking at the Friends entering the Meetinghouse one by one, Elizabeth was hopeful that more progress could be made about John Hoffman's bequest. She had spoken at great length earlier in the day with Bill about the matter. With his approval, she was going to begin the Meeting with an explanation of the plans John had recorded in his journal.

"Friends, we have two unusual circumstances we need to confront in connection with John's death. His was not a natural death, and, so far, the person responsible for his killing has not come forward. John's will, recorded some years ago, is a fairly traditional one and leaves this Meeting one hundred thousand dollars to do with as it wishes. The fact that the money comes to us directly because of extreme violence needs to be faced. Also, we can be sure that had John lived a bit longer, little of his money would have come to us. John's nephew and lawyer, Bill Hoffman, can explain what was in John's mind."

Bill rose and took some papers out of his pocket. Looking tense and serious, he glanced briefly around the room as if to confirm that he had everyone's attention. Then he cleared his throat and began.

"Just before my uncle's death, he was going through a period of deep change. We all remember what he said about the evil he thought was inherent in wealth when he spoke in Meeting for Worship the last Sunday he was alive. Just after Meeting, he gave these papers to me, with instructions to divide up his considerable estate among several different organizations, including soup kitchens in this country and a university in El Salvador. It was an unusual request, certainly, and because of my own narrowness I opposed it. My uncle was killed before the matter was resolved.

"John Hoffman kept a detailed journal all of his adult life. The most recent volume of that journal I couldn't bring with me tonight, but it describes the spiritual journey he was making and what that meant for his finances. It's clear from the journal and from what he said to me that he was earnest about giving away all his estate. I'm still not sure how he would have lived after doing that, but that didn't seem to concern him. Perhaps that concerned me too much. Although it does still seem to me his old age needed to be provided for. I'm just not sure.

"But I think Friends can be confident that John's changes in this regard were Spirit-led and that if he had been closer to any of us, we would've understood a lot more about what he was being called to do. Even I, his nearest relative, didn't talk in a serious way with my uncle. And I think it's a criticism of our community that John could have worked long and hard on such important issues without the involvement of other members in the process. But I think it's also true that my uncle could've been better at allowing other people into his life." Here Bill paused and closed his eyes for a moment. He leaned slightly forward, opened his eyes, and continued.

"The way I see the problem is this. My uncle's intentions were different from what's now the only legal possibility open to us. He intended substantial gifts to a variety of groups that aren't the ones traditionally supported by Quaker businesspeople. The Meeting will get one hundred thousand dollars from John, however, because that's the way the will reads and the way the law works. I will inherit the bulk of my uncle's estate, because that's what his will indicates. For my part, I plan to give what I receive from my uncle's estate to the Catholic Worker and to the soup kitchen here in our neighborhood at Christ Church. I've written today to those organizations to explain that they can expect a substantial gift from me in the near future. If the Meeting gave what it will receive to American University in El Salvador, the university that supported the priests whom the military killed last fall, I think that we Friends would be acting in keeping with my uncle's wishes."

Bill sat down. No one but Elizabeth and Patience, and possibly Adam, could have anticipated the information that Bill had given the Meeting. The silence of Meeting was complete. Even Hugo Coleman, so often quick to speak where the group's finances were concerned, did not look like he was ready to rise. Elizabeth thought for a moment about how a Clerk might handle a development like this. She decided to speak.

"Friends, this is new information. It may be unusual for a Friend my age to reconsider some of the basic questions of life, but I'm sure it may be a possibility for all of us, even when our hair is gray. I've read John's journal and am convinced that his decision was led by the Spirit. Meeting may be legally entitled to the one hundred thousand dollars, but Quakers have never been known for legalisms. Perhaps the Peace and Social Concerns Committee could help us to understand some of what has recently been happening in El Salvador so that we could feel a connection to the university there to which this money should go."

A few minutes of silence passed, and then Patience Silverstone slowly rose to her feet. "As someone even older than John and Elizabeth, I would like to say that we ancients really can think, feel, and find new paths to God. We all know what a serious person John Hoffman was. John's journey on financial questions deserves our respect. Let us honor his memory and his wishes by committing the money we will receive to the organization he felt called to support. God bless him and help us to follow his example."

Patience sat down slowly, her stiff joints almost audibly creaking. After a moment Hugo Coleman stood and simply said, "That Friend speaks my mind." The sense of the Meeting was clear to all, and Elizabeth began to close the Meeting. But Bill Hoffman was again on his feet, asking if he might speak. The Clerk was startled but recognized him. Bill stood even more awkwardly than before, slowly shifting his weight from one foot to another. He ran his hand through his hair twice and then began.

"Friends, a lot of grief can be avoided when we're honest with one another. I know better than most that honesty can be difficult, and on some questions it's easy to remain silent so as not to disturb other people's peace. But several events have made it clear to me that the time for silence is past in my life. Even though I now hope to become a judge, an appointment I have looked forward to for a long time, and even though the political process involved in confirmation has its risks for me, I want to speak honestly with my Meeting tonight. I hope you'll listen as patiently as you can to what I have to say.

"Since I was a child I have struggled to understand why and how I am so different from most of you. For a long time I feared my difference might lead to my leaving the Meeting, but I've been sure for a long time now that that isn't the case, and I hope Meeting will agree with me. I've been gay for as long as I've known myself, and it is a difficult burden to bear. Unfortunately, it's a heavy burden even in our Society, and that's what I want to speak to tonight. There are several respected Friends whose sexual orientation isn't known to Meeting because they fear the condemnation that might follow disclosure. I surely understand that. I remember some of the things I was taught in Meeting as a child, the homophobia behind several of the lessons I was given. Straight Friends cannot imagine the hurt this causes, the lifelong pain that such teachings inspire. Can we ever recover from our childhoods, spent in Quaker Meeting and in Quaker families?" Bill stopped and again ran a hand through his hair. A grimace was now on his face and he bit his lip. Then he continued, his voice rising in pitch.

"It isn't clear to me that we really can. The anger that is in us runs deep, and I hope that Friends will find the strength required to listen to us, even listening through our anger as best we can. My uncle was perhaps the worst offender in Meeting about not listening on this question, and I feel free to say so as his relative. I now understand the last part of his life was spent more deeply in the Spirit than I have ever been, and I envy him that, but on all questions concerning gay life he was, as we know, a closed and narrow man.

"I decided when we sat down for this Meeting tonight that I wouldn't go home until I had spoken on this point. I know there's been too much dishonesty in my life on this matter, and I want all that to change now. I certainly appreciate what energy is required of Friends to listen to one of the gay community."

Bill sat down abruptly. Elizabeth was conscious of a new pain in her head, and she took a moment to rub her temples. Bill's anger had been clear. She could respect it in some ways, but as a Clerk she resented that he had steered a Business Meeting on to a topic of his own, rather than the group's, choosing. She wondered what to do now, and whether she should simply close the Meeting where it stood. As she thought about this she saw Patience again rising slowly to her feet.

"Thee hast spoken unexpectedly tonight, Friend," she said, nodding in Bill's direction, "and I doubt that Meeting can respond properly at this time to all thee hast said. I'm deeply glad that thee spoke, since all honesty can only lead us into the Light. And I think we will try to listen. But listening is always a two-way street. John Hoffman was an outspoken man at the end of his life, but his thinking is shared by several of us. We can only find God's will through mutual understanding. Perhaps the Clerk and Ministry and Council can consider ways we can address this matter more directly in the future rather than in this large Business Meeting format."

Elizabeth thought this a sound suggestion and asked all present to hold this issue in their prayers as she would. She then closed the Meeting. As Friends rose to go home, several people went to Bill and spoke in quiet tones with him. Hugo Coleman and Wally Orvick were conferring in one corner of the room, still thinking about the money issues decided tonight. Elizabeth went over to Patience and helped her get her coat on, thanking her for speaking on both questions that had been addressed.

"I know you generally don't have the energy to come to these evening Meetings, but I'm grateful you came tonight."

"I'm glad I was here. Would thee walk me home? I have trouble with the old uneven sidewalks in the dark."

Patience and Elizabeth walked out into the night together.

It was cold, and because Patience walked slowly, both women had time to feel the wind cutting through the warmth of their coats. Elizabeth was nearly shivering when

Patience said, "William would make a fine judge, I think. He has gone through tribulation now and is coming out on the far side of pain and wrongdoing. I assume that thee and I have had the whole truth from him."

"I hope so."

There was a long pause. The elderly Quaker almost stumbled on a small drop in the brick sidewalk. The city of Cambridge did not keep things in repair as it might, and the roots of ancient trees and the action of the frost combined to make some sections of sidewalk into undulating ribbons of worn brick.

"I doubt anyone is born with a judicial temperament," Patience continued as they neared her house. "It must be acquired. William may be in the process of learning how to judge others as he looks at his own life. So we can hope."

"Yes," readily answered the Clerk. She saw Patience into her front door and then stepped more quickly through the darkness toward Concord Avenue and home.

Shortly after lunch on Thursday Elizabeth Elliot received a telephone call from Stewart Burnham.

"I'm calling partly by way of apology, Mrs. Elliot," began the detective. "You were right about Tim Schouweiler's story, as far as we can tell. We let him out on Monday, as you may know. And the victim's nephew has come forward with some information he'd been holding back on us. He told me you had a lot to do with his coming forward."

"No, it was his own conscience at work."

"That's not the way he put it. Anyway, I wanted to thank you for the help you've been." The detective's tone was more strained as he added, "Could I ask what you think of Bill Hoffman's story? You've known him a long time, I gather. This alibi of his could have been arranged."

"I'm not sure what you mean by 'arranged,' Mr. Burnham," Elizabeth answered slowly. "I have no reason to think James Reynolds is a liar. Bill certainly did some lying to us all about the events of that Monday. But he may be telling the whole truth now. The way I see it, the truth will come out. It's only a matter of time now. Bill is thinking hard about lots of things, and good things will come of the changes within him. He truly may have told us everything already."

"Yes, he may. Then again, he may not. But if you don't have a clear feeling about it, that's the way it is. Again, thanks for your help with the Schouweiler situation."

Elizabeth accepted the thanks, deciding against lecturing the detective on his bigotries concerning the homeless and his less-than-legal ways of gathering evidence against them. She and Burnham said good-bye and hung up.

On Friday afternoon Elizabeth was putting some dried peas to soak for soup. She had spent the morning on household tasks, glad to have a break from the problems of the Meeting. It had been a productive day. The ringing telephone interrupted her. Harriet was on the line.

"I'm not sure what to do, Friend," said Harriet in a whisper.

"I can barely hear you."

"But I can't speak more loudly. You know the homeless man who often comes here. Tim. He's here now and says he has to speak to you. I didn't want to tell him where you lived. These men can be hard to get rid of. So he says he'll stay right here until you come. There's no shaking him."

"I'm glad he's still in the neighborhood. If I had been held in jail for as long as he was, when they let me out I'd run for Maine."

"But what should I do?"

"Tell him I'll be right down, of course! I'll be there in ten minutes."

Elizabeth was as good as her word. She arrived a little breathless, but shook hands with Tim, who was sitting outside Harriet's door.

"Come into the kitchen, Friend," said the Clerk to the disheveled young man. "Shall I put on hot water? We can have tea."

"I don't drink tea."

"Well, would instant coffee be OK? We have that, too."

"Yeah."

Tim sat down at the table in the big kitchen as Elizabeth put the kettle on the stove.

"I'm glad to see you're in one piece. That much time in jail would drive me bonkers, I think."

"It's a shitty place."

"What's on your mind now?"

"You still interested in who killed John Hoffman?"

Elizabeth nodded her head.

"It was the other Hoffman in your congregation. The younger one. I was wandering around Longfellow Park at lunchtime that Sunday. Adam spoke to me here and I wanted to get away from him, so I was just stretching my legs. I came on the Hoffmans, down by the statue of Longfellow. John was saying those same things he'd said at Meeting. He was a hypocrite. Saying how blessed it was to give. We hear a lot of that on the streets. It's all bullshit, I tell you."

The kettle boiled. Elizabeth made a cup of instant coffee and handed it to Tim while he continued.

"I can pretty much remember the exact words. John was saying he didn't need money anymore. He had been freed from all that. And the other Hoffman said, 'You expect me to take care of you in your old age! I won't, I tell you. I'm going to have less money from now on and I sure as hell won't spend any on you! You ought to die now if you're going to be a burden to us all.' "

Tim sipped the coffee noisily and asked if there was cream and sugar. Elizabeth could find no cream in the refrigerator, but she provided him with a bowl of sugar from which he liberally helped himself.

"It stuck in my mind because you Quakers aren't much for shouting, but that younger Hoffman was really scream-ing. He was yelling right in John's face. I thought he might hit the old guy right there, so I sort of casually walked away. It wasn't my fight, you know?"

"No, it wasn't," said Elizabeth. "It's sad to think two such good men would be reduced to that. And on First-day!"

"So it maybe was the other Hoffman who killed John. See?"

"Yes, I see your point. At the moment, I don't think it would help anybody for you to tell the police what you heard. But of course that's up to you. And maybe it's right to tell them everything."

"Hell, no, you got me wrong. I don't talk to those mo-therfuckers. They wouldn't believe me anyway. Like your secretary here wouldn't believe that I know you and might have a good reason for talking to you. Same mind-set. But I thought you might want to know, seeing the interest you've taken in that stuff."

Tim rose and walked out of the kitchen without another word. Elizabeth saw him go out the front door of the build-ing and disappear in the direction of Harvard Square.

Saturday afternoon traffic was only moderately heavy as Elizabeth walked through Harvard Square toward her house. She was returning home after a morning appointment with her doctor to adjust her prescribed blood pressure medication. Her doctor, as old as she, was one of the few left in Cambridge who would see anyone on a Saturday.

She hoped the traffic was a fair imitation of what the streets had been like on the afternoon of Columbus Day. She returned to her home on Concord Avenue, looked at the clock, and waited in her living room. She stood at the front window. After a bit she went to the kitchen and put on water for tea, then returned to her vantage point at the window. The water boiled, the tea was made and stored in a Thermos. Elizabeth returned to her post.

Soon she saw them, pedalling vigorously up Concord Avenue, Sarah in front and apparently setting the pace, Steven a little behind. Elizabeth went to the front door and opened it. As she walked down the steps, she smiled at the picture her niece made with her boyfriend. Both were young, strong, and enjoying themselves.

Sarah reached Elizabeth's curb a moment before Steven and called out, "Hi, Aunt Elizabeth! Did we do OK?"

Elizabeth smiled again and looked at her watch.

Sarah was getting off her bike and breathing hard. She held out her watch for Elizabeth to see, saying, "We left just when you said; it's only sixteen minutes to here." Sarah stopped for a moment for several gulps of air, then continued, "We did push ourselves a little, I admit, but not too badly."

Steven, just arriving, was breathing even more deeply and was red in the face. The cool autumn wind that was blowing up the street would quickly chill both sweaty bikers, Elizabeth thought, with motherly concern. Steven, unaware he was the object of worry, smiled and dismounted with a bit of style. Elizabeth introduced herself while Sarah locked both bikes.

"I've good tea made," Elizabeth said.

"I told you that we'd at least get tea out of this!" said Sarah gaily to her friend. Both young people came inside, where their hostess served tea and spice cookies.

"Did you begin at Park Street station?" asked Elizabeth.

"Yes," answered Steven. "That's what Sarah said you wanted us to do. We were delayed for one minute just after we got over the Charles by three fire trucks that came roaring by."

"Steve pulled over to the side of the street, like you're supposed to do, but I kept going in the interests of timing the trip better. I always put science over safety," said Sarah. She was on her fourth cookie as she added, "It took you quite a while to catch up to me, mad dog."

Steven looked at Elizabeth and said, "Sarah will get herself killed someday, the way she bikes. But anyway, it takes a little under twenty minutes to get here." Both young people were relaxing now with refilled cups.

"Thank you both for doing the experiment," said Elizabeth. "I could never have done it myself."

"What's the big mystery about? Can't you tell us now why we did this?" asked Sarah.

"I'll fill you both in on everything when the matter is settled. Meeting life has its complexities at the moment."

"Well," responded Steven, "it all sounds more intriguing than Hillel life. We've never had much to investigate."

"Sarah tells me you are one of the organizers of your services," said Elizabeth. Steven nodded. "I'm afraid the only Jewish service I ever went to was a wedding, and that was at least forty years ago."

"Things have changed a lot since then, at least in most Jewish circles. All I do at Hillel is read on Friday evenings, and I'm one of the people who sells tickets for the High Holidays."

Elizabeth was puzzled by the notion of tickets to a religious event. She wondered if asking questions was a good thing or if it would embarrass her niece. Because both Sarah and Steven seemed at ease she ventured, "Are tickets normally part of the arrangements for the fall holidays?"

"Oh, yes," answered Steven, a bit startled that that had not been clear. "In most temples seating is really a problem for those services. Having a ticket is the only way to guarantee you can get in."

"And it's also a big money raiser," added Sarah.

This, too, was a new concept to Elizabeth. It occurred to her as she sat looking at her two young guests that she really knew nothing of religious practices outside of Quakerism.

Steven continued, "The tickets are priced high. It's the only way to force some financial responsibility on people. That reminds me, when I visited your service the other Sunday, no one passed a plate to take money."

"No," said Elizabeth, "we don't have an offering plate. Our attitudes about that may be peculiar. Many Quakers think all we can manage to do together is silent prayer. Straying beyond that in any way is suspect."

"How do you raise money for the group?" asked Steven, shaking his head to the gestured offer of a third cup of tea.

"We use subtle pressure, I think," said Sarah. "Giving lots of money to the Meeting is considered a good thing; it's something people can be proud of. Supposedly giving is a private matter, but people who give a lot find a way to let people know how generous they are. Wealthy Quakers are quite good at a quiet sort of bragging."

"To be slightly less cynical about it," added Sarah's aunt, "wealthy Friends can be important to the budget, but giving is considered a matter between you and your conscience, just like everything else. Things have gone downhill about giving in recent years, I must admit. In the old days all Quakers tithed to their local Meetings. 'Offerings' were everything given beyond the tithe."

"An idea you must have picked up from us," said Steven with a smile.

"Exactly," responded Elizabeth. "But in these late days, I'm afraid, few people tithe. A lot of money is given by just a handful of well-to-do Quakers. That's certainly true in Cambridge Meeting."

"And the bad thing about that," said Sarah, "is that the people who contribute a lot can exercise a lot of influence in Meeting for Business, where the decisions get made. At least about financial questions, like redoing the building."

"I don't think that it's true that the wealthy people control our decisions, Sarah. That's meant to be a matter of the Spirit leading the congregation, and I think it often really is a Spirit-led process."

"Yes, I'm sure it is, sometimes," replied Sarah, "but that's not to say that if someone like me shows up for Business Meeting and speaks on a particular issue that Friends would listen to me as carefully as they do to someone like that man who got murdered."

Elizabeth considered before responding, "Actually, if you ever came to Business Meeting, I for one would listen carefully to anything you said. You've never come, have you?"

"Ouch!" responded her niece. "You're right, of course. I don't even make it to worship every Sunday."

"John Woolman was well on his way to becoming a Recorded Minister when he was your age," said Elizabeth in a severe Quaker tone, "and I'm sure his Meeting listened seriously to what he had to say. Youth and poverty are no obstacles to Quaker ministry, Sarah."

"OK," said Sarah. "I'm sorry. I'm in no position to criticize anyway, since I can hardly be called an active Quaker."

There was a strained pause in the conversation. Steven broke it by asking for more tea. Since he had earlier declined another cup, Elizabeth noted him down as a polite young man with some social skills. She refilled his cup and hers and turned the conversation back to Hillel life.

"I remember back when I was in school, shortly after the dinosaurs died out, that the Jewish kids had trouble during the High Holidays in the fall. School was on and attendance was required for those days, just like any other."

"At Harvard it's still a little bit like that," answered Steven, "but most profs will let you out of labs and things if you ask. It's a hassle not fitting in with the Christian calendar, but it's not one of our biggest problems." He turned and looked at his girlfriend as he added, "As I've said to Sarah, if she converted, she'd get more holidays as a Jew than as a Quaker."

"That's right, I guess," said Sarah, "but if you were to convert you could finally celebrate Christmas, which is one of the best holidays around."

"One of the most gaudy, certainly," said Elizabeth. "It's a shame that the Christmas celebration is one of the best-known things about Christianity."

"That's a bit the way I feel about the High Holidays," said Steven. "They're not what being a Jew is about, day by day, but they're the things most non-Jews know about us."

"Another thing I know, or think I know, about Jews is the important place that women can have in religious life. The Friday evening meal and prayer, for example." Steven nodded his head and Elizabeth continued, "Sarah was telling me that a child's identity as a Jew really depends on the child's mother rather than his father."

"That's right," said Steven. "A Jew is a Jew if his mother is a Jew. I can become a citizen of Israel because my mother is a Jew. It really doesn't matter if my father was or not."

"But that's not the same as women's liberation, Aunt," said Sarah quickly. "Steve thinks I should convert and become a Jew. He doesn't offer to join Quakerism but expects me to join his religion. In my women's studies class we have several words to describe that attitude."

Steven laughed and replied, "I only want you to convert because my family and I happen to be in the right group!"

Sarah was not laughing. She looked at her watch and visibly pulled herself together. Then she smiled at her aunt and thanked her for the cookies and tea.

"Of course," said Elizabeth, wondering if Sarah wished to stop what could have been a serious discussion. Sarah rose to go and gave Steven a significant look. He politely thanked Elizabeth for her hospitality.

"Not at all," she answered, "it's I who must thank both of you for making that bike trip for me. I appreciate the time and sweat involved. I could never have done it."

She took the young people back to the front door where they put on their jackets and gloves and said good-bye. Elizabeth watched them unlock their bikes and pedal off down Concord Avenue in the direction of Harvard.

11

Prayer is the aspiration of the soul. It is man's communion with God and is an essential to religious life. The result of prayer becomes apparent in the nobler lives of those who are constant in its exercise. We, individually, should cultivate the habit of turning to God at all times, and of seeking Divine guidance in all things that we may, in truth, be led by Him. Vocal prayer, when prompted by a deep concern and a sense of human need, is a vital part of public worship and often helps those assembled to come into the consciousness of God's presence.

New York Yearly Meeting, 1950

Elizabeth Elliot waited sadly but calmly for Adam to arrive. Sparkle waited with her, sensing her mistress's tension and, for once, not abandoning her for the refuge of the basement. With Sparkle to stroke and the birds outside to watch, Elizabeth waited as patiently as she could. She reviewed the last several weeks as she patted the cat. She had learned much about several members of the Meeting. Many of the things which had come to light, she wished she might never have known. From what she could tell, secrecy, fear, and anger were woven into the fabric of life. At the age of sixty-six, Elizabeth realized that this should no longer surprise her. Still, there is always a part of us that denies wrongdoing and evil, and that is deeply hurt by the experience of disillusionment. Perhaps it was the disillusionment that made the grace of God all the more miraculous to her. She thought of grace as that which redeems life from itself.

When Adam arrived at Elizabeth's door he looked exhausted, and pain was evident on his face. The doorbell had sent Sparkle scurrying for the basement, but even the neurotic cat seemed calm in comparison to Adam. Elizabeth saw that he had locked his bike around the mailbox at her front door. She asked him to come in from the raw cold and said that they both seemed in need of tea. Adam said nothing, but came in and sat down heavily at the kitchen table.

Elizabeth heated water, put a pot of tea on the table, and began her story gently. As she sipped her tea she explained Tim's movements on the Monday afternoon of Columbus Day and her ability to verify all parts of his story.

"I think we can both be glad he's in the clear, Adam, since many in this society would find it easy to blame him. Indeed, many in our own Society would feel comfortable with the idea that he was the killer, instead of one of us. I'm sure you can feel some of my relief that he won't be hounded further."

"Yes. Of course you're right, Friend; it's good that he's beyond suspicion," responded Adam. He stared down at his teacup without drinking.

"Erik Swensen's business affairs were in disarray, and that would've come to John Hoffman's attention soon, had John lived," said Elizabeth. "It seems that Erik's dealing with savings and loans around town had gotten him into an insoluble mess. And he was certainly in trouble with the law. He was under investigation by the federal authorities when he died. His suicide note makes it clear he knew he was guilty of fraud."

"Perhaps one might argue that Erik couldn't bear for John to know of his errors at work," she continued, "but I believe Erik's story of where he was on that Monday afternoon, and were he the murderer, he probably wouldn't have gone to John's house on Tuesday morning. Still, I suppose some killers might be bold enough to do that. But John's death accelerated the financial disaster that was coming down on Erik Swensen. John's influence and connections would have been helpful in saving the business had the partnership continued. John's good judgment had never been called into question. Erik lost by John's death."

Elizabeth finished her tea and poured another cup.

"Perhaps Erik could kill in anger or in self-defense, but he certainly wouldn't have killed John Hoffman in a premeditated way. I believe he liked and respected John and was shocked by his death. Erik's suicide message confesses to a lot, but it doesn't mention John's death at all.

"There is, of course, Bill Hoffman to consider," continued Elizabeth. "You and I and the rest of the Meeting heard John tell us he was going to alter his financial affairs in a major way. Had he lived, I'm sure he would've done so, although I'm not absolutely sure how. It's never easy for the rich to divest themselves of their property, especially those who have earned the money by their own labor. But Bill Hoffman might reasonably expect he would no longer be his uncle's main heir, and clearly that meant the loss of a great deal of money.

"Your tea will soon be cold, Adam. Have a fresh cupful that's hot. Drink it down. It will do you good," said Elizabeth.

"No, I think I'm past feeling much pain now, Friend. Please continue," answered Adam.

"On that last Sunday of John's life we all saw the anger in Tim about what John had said in Meeting for Worship. But my niece tells me someone else was angry with John. She saw John and another man in Longfellow Park in a heated argument. Sarah doesn't distinguish very much among people over thirty in Meeting, and she paid no attention to who the other man in the argument was. But Tim Schouweiler is an observant man. He came to me after he got out of jail and told me what he had seen and heard that lunchtime. He saw John and his nephew walk away into the park, and he could see they were arguing with each other. Bill was pushing away something John was trying to give him, and he shouted at his uncle. That fits with what Bill has told Patience and me about that day. He wasn't honest when I first spoke to him, but he seems to be now.

"Bill's account of his movements has changed. He's not innocent of wrongdoing by any means: he hid John's journal before the police might have taken an interest in it. If Bill were his uncle's murderer, his behavior since the time of John's death has been that of calling attention to the guilty. When I confronted Bill about his removing evidence he broke down. He has an alibi from four to six that afternoon. He was with a man from Harvard." She paused and then added, "Not a Meeting member. Whatever some of us may think of his private life, and whatever Patience and I think of his initial deceit, it's clear to me that Bill Hoffman is guilty of no violence."

Elizabeth paused again briefly, said a small prayer, looked up at Adam, and continued:

"I can't appreciate all you must feel. But it's time we all faced the truth. You say you couldn't have been at John's house in the late afternoon. But accepting your story about the demonstration doesn't preclude your going to Royal Avenue. Chris Richardson told me she saw you locking up your bike when you arrived at the demonstration that afternoon. She didn't think anything of that—you often bike around town—but it means you had your bike with you, something you were careful not to tell me.

"My niece Sarah and a friend of hers bicycled from city hall, near the Park Street station in Boston, to John's house on Royal Avenue for me. They took the route I told them to: up Cambridge Street to the Harvard area and then up Concord Avenue. It took them fifteen minutes or so. Because John's death was on Columbus Day, the street traffic would have been a bit light and you could have done it quickly, just like them. Maybe you did try to take the train, and that's how you came to know it was out of service. You were quick to mention to me that the trains were not running that day. But it's not a long trip for a strong man on a good bike, is it?"

Adam answered, "I biked to the protest; you're right. I thought if the demo was a fizzle, which happens a lot, people are so apathetic, I'd bike on to the arboretum. But the turnout at city hall was good, and I stayed most of the afternoon. When I left the demo a bit before five and was unlocking my bike, I overheard a couple of businessmen types complaining that the Red Line was out of commission. I kept my appointment for five P.M. with John by biking straight across town. The traffic is pretty hairy on the bridge, but it's not far from here to downtown as the crow flies.

"Your niece must be a pretty fearless biker, by the way. The trip took me at least twenty-five minutes."

Elizabeth looked at Adam and gently continued.

"Something must have happened when you talked to John, something I can only guess at. You two were out in the back garden. You argued. You fell or he fell. You hit him with the spade that was lying there where he'd been working. But why, Adam, why such anger?"

"It was his doing, not mine!" answered Adam. "I went there to speak to him about the Business Meeting and what he had said the previous day. The gay community in the Meeting has been patient with us, but from their perspective it's easy to imagine that someone like John Hoffman would stand in their way forever! John didn't even talk to the gays. Or even to you and me, Elizabeth—about that issue, I mean. He should've spoken to us from his heart and not just remain silent for two years until we neared a decision. He kept to himself for years, but then felt free to block the progress that we were finally making. I wanted to explain to him how his behavior looks to the gays and lesbians in Meeting, and I wanted to show him, if I could, that homosexuality wasn't something he needed to be revolted by. I was sure he was better than he sounded on Sunday afternoon, if he only would have thought!"

"Absolutely," agreed Elizabeth softly. "We all improve when we think."

"When I got to his house, just about five o'clock, I suppose, there was no answer at the door. So I went around back, where he works in the garden. Sure enough, he was there. I leaned my bike up against the house and walked over to where he was working. We chatted for a little while about this and that, and then I brought up the subject of same-sex marriage. He got serious and then angry as we talked. I said I thought his emotions were based on ignorance and bigotry, not on the gospel."

"Strong words," said Elizabeth quietly.

"Yes, but they're true words, Elizabeth! He was an ignorant bigot! I said that I thought his attitude was all the more strange since his nephew was gay. He exploded and shouted that I was lying. I said I certainly wasn't lying, Bill made no secret of it to me when this same-sex question first came up. Bill has not fully 'come out,' but I thought his uncle was aware. John denied it again and again, and I shouted at him that he should talk to Bill. Then I made a real mistake, I know that now. I said that some gays never recognize their own sexuality because society represses it in them so much, and the Society of Friends does that, too. And I added that his revulsion at the idea of the Meeting doing same-sex marriages might come from denial in his own life.

"He turned purple in the face and grabbed me by the throat. He was amazingly strong for a guy his age, but then he still works out on the river. He tried to choke me, and I fell over backward with him on top. I had hit my head when I fell, I guess, because I was really woozy. He grabbed me around the neck again. I couldn't breathe and I was almost blacking out. We rolled in the dirt, and the next thing I knew my hand was against a spade or something. I grabbed it and hit him on the shoulder. He eased his grip on my neck, and my head started to clear a little. He reached for my throat again, and I hit him on the head. I think I hit him one more time, I'm not sure. I just wanted him to stop choking me. He was killing me, Elizabeth! By the time my hand found that shovel I was just like a machine, hitting him to try to save my life.

"He stopped moving and we both lay there in the dirt for quite a long time, me getting my breath back again and John dying. When I could sit up, I did. I realized then what I had done, and the horror of it hit me. I just ran, Elizabeth. It was like I was on autopilot. I ran to my bike, I got on it, and I rode away as fast as I could. The fear was overwhelming. I know that's no excuse. I'm just saying I never felt anything like it. I rode toward Harvard Square without thinking. When I did think I realized that I should make as good an alibi for myself as I could.

"I ditched my bike in the Square, took a taxi to the Beacon Hill Meeting, and told the people there I had just come from the demo. That was just about the time the demo was officially meant to break up, you see. I sat inside for a little bit before speaking to anyone, and then I let on I'd been there quite a while, warming up. I was having some trouble speaking, because of the choking and all, but I told them there that I'd been shouting all afternoon at the demo and that had made my voice hoarse."

"When I called you on Tuesday I remember your voice was hardly recognizable," said Elizabeth.

"Yes. My neck and throat were in bad shape. I wore turtlenecks to cover the bruises for the next two weeks."

"I noticed the turtleneck you wore at the memorial Meeting; it wasn't the sort of thing you normally wear."

"Anyway, when John's death was discovered I was still in shock. Then the whole investigation began, and piecing things together I realized that Bill and Erik Swensen both had motives for murder, of a sort, and so did Tim. So I hoped that nobody would be singled out. Would that have been so bad, Elizabeth? Did anyone need to be convicted of this? Do you think that's justice? I just couldn't face telling you and the Meeting what I had done; I still want to deny that I struck him. But after he grabbed my throat and started choking me, I reacted like a robot."

"No one in Meeting who hasn't been through the same thing is in a position to judge or condemn your behavior," said Elizabeth, "although I suppose not all Friends will see it that way."

"I ran, I was afraid for my life, and I lied to you and the police. It was all wrong."

"Yes, it was wrong," responded the Clerk. "But anyone in such a circumstance would be afraid. I'm not saying any of what you did was OK, but I am saying this Quaker does not condemn what was done in panic."

Adam sobbed, reached for Elizabeth's hand, sobbed again, and said, "What can I do? I know things can't be right ever again, but what can I do now?"

"I'm no priest to give penances to you, and I can't give absolution. God is the source of grace, Adam, not me nor the Meeting. Nor the police nor the law. But God does not forget His children."

Adam let go of Elizabeth's hand, put his face down on the table, and sobbed.

"I'm a terrible failure."

"No! I'm sure you're not. None of us is. There is no such thing as failure in this world, Friend. There is suffering. There is certainly death. But we can't fail as God's creatures, not in the end. We suffer when we are far from God, when we can't see Him, but that's all there is: our suffering.

"No one would choose to go through what you went

through that day and in the days since then. Your suffering is enough without these nightmares of failure," said Elizabeth.

Adam sobbed, but more quietly. She took his hand, and the two of them sat for quite a long time. Elizabeth prayed. After a while Adam looked up, dried his face on his sleeves, and said, "I think I'll go to the police and tell them what happened."

Elizabeth looked at his drawn features and tearstained face and said, "That seems like the best thing now, I think, for you and also for the other men who have been suspected. I'll call Detective Burnham from here, if you want, and he can send a car."

"Will you keep my bike for me?"

"Gladly," responded Elizabeth. "I'll keep it inside the house until you return."

"That might be a long time, Elizabeth," answered Adam as he rose from his chair.

"I'll keep it until you return, Friend," she reiterated. "God willing, the police will listen to your evidence. I don't know the law, but we can hope that self-defense is a plea that courts understand. And we'll get you good legal advice. Bill will do that much for us."

She stood up from the table, went into the hallway, and dialed Detective Burnham's number.

Elizabeth cleared away the cold teapot and the dirty cups from the kitchen table. Burnham had come promptly to her house and in half a dozen words asked Adam to come down to the station before making any statement. The two men had departed so quickly that Elizabeth had not properly said good-bye to Adam. She called Bill Hoffman and explained the situation. He promised to get one of his lawyer friends to go down to the police station right away and be with Adam when he was questioned.

As the sun set in Cambridge, Elizabeth took a pot roast and potatoes out of the refrigerator and put them on the stove top to heat. Her son Andrew, the engineer, had given her a microwave the previous year, but it remained in its box in the basement. She had not yet overcome her fear of technological change in the kitchen. As her supper warmed in the steamer on the stove, she turned on National Public Radio. She did not hear a word of the news as she absentmindedly put down food for Sparkle, who, as usual, was nowhere to be seen. Although she was lost in thought about Adam, it did not take her long to dispatch her modest meal. As she was washing up, the doorbell rang. It was Sarah Curtis, standing in the darkness on the front steps, her face stained with tears.

"Come in, come in," said Elizabeth before her niece had a chance to speak. Sarah entered, struggled out of her jacket, and blurted, "Oh, Aunt, I'm sorry to barge in on you! Especially when I'm in such a state."

"Not at all! Come into the living room."

Elizabeth turned on all the lights, fetched a box of tissues from her desk in the corner and placed it on the coffee table at Sarah's elbow, and turned up the thermostat while Sarah caught her breath. When the elderly Quaker sat down on the sofa, her niece was ready to speak.

"Steve and I went out for pizza after leaving here. We often do on Saturday evening. Since we were on our bikes, we went down to the Bertucci's near MIT. It's less crowded than the one here."

Elizabeth nodded.

"He started talking about our future. And now it's clear what he expects of me. He says we'll need to live in Boston until he's finished with law school. Yesterday he learned he's been admitted to Harvard Law, you see. We've talked about this before, but I've never said for sure that I was willing to stay here. A year from now I'll be applying to medical schools. At least I think so. And there's no telling where I'll be admitted and where I'll end up going."

Again Elizabeth silently nodded.

"But Steve just assumes that because he's been admitted to Harvard Law, I have to stay here." Tears crept from Sarah's eyes as she continued. "I'm afraid I got pretty angry with him. I told him he was thinking like a chauvinist. He clearly didn't care about my education and career, at least not compared to his. So he acted really hurt and said of course he cared, but there are several medical schools here in town. That's true, but it's not the point. He assumes that what's best for him is best for me."

Elizabeth sat forward in her chair. Her face was held in a frown as she said, "I think that was roughly your uncle Michael's attitude in our marriage. But there was no other way of thinking when we were young and were making decisions about schooling."

"I'm sure it's still my father's attitude, too. My mother has never gotten to pursue her own life. Quakers talk a lot about women's equality, but you sure don't see real respect for women in the attitudes of men around Meeting."

"Sometimes I'm afraid that's true," replied Elizabeth cautiously. "Although I think we do better than some groups."

"Anyway, the pizza came, but I didn't have the stomach for it. I told Steve this law school stuff was just as bad as his attitudes about religion. He assumes I'll eventually convert, because he's a man and I'm a woman. Actually, in some ways I wouldn't mind the change. There's a lot to be said for the Jewish tradition from what I can see at Hillel. But he shouldn't *assume* I have to change!

"Last week he quoted the 'Wither thou goes, I will go, and your God will be my God' verse from the Old Testament at me. Like any good Quaker kid, I know that's what the woman is supposed to say. But the verse was written several thousand years ago! Times change!"

"Times are changing," said Elizabeth, "but all social changes are slow and difficult. Many Quaker young men expect about the same from their young women, just like your father and my Michael did. At least that's what they expect and want unconsciously, whatever they say on First-day."

"It's not good enough for me!" said Sarah angrily. "I'll read Virginia Woolf when I want and I'll go to medical school where I want. Steven can drown himself in the Charles!"

"Your anger is understandable," said Elizabeth quietly. "But it may pass in time. You do like him, after all, and that means he has real virtues."

"Yes, he does. But my life is my own and I have to live it for myself. Not for someone else. That's what he doesn't seem to understand."

"He may come to understand it in time," replied Elizabeth. She paused. "It could be that it's beyond him, I suppose. Can you be OK with or without him?"

"Yes," answered Sarah calmly and certainly.

"Good," replied her aunt. "That's the important thing."

12

Our life is love, and peace, and tenderness; and bearing one with another, and forgiving one another, and not laying accusations one against another; but praying one for another, and helping one another up with a tender hand.

Isaac Penington, 1667

At dawn, the sunlight of the last Sunday in October is clear. The clouds are high and air pollution is slight. The streets of Cambridge gradually awaken. The subway system disgorges people into Harvard Square. They buy their morning coffee and watch chess players, wrapped up against the chill, pair up for games on the sidewalk at tables provided for this purpose. The homeless, who have spent the night in the square, sit around the subway entrances asking passersby for change. As time passes, the homeless are almost lost in the many people who pass through Harvard Square on a Sunday morning. Pious Cambridgians on their way to church contribute to the scene. They walk to Christ Church, to Old Cambridge Baptist Church, to St. Paul's Church, to University Lutheran Church, the Church of England Monastery, and the Mormon Mission Church.

Tim Schouweiler, who has spent the night on the heating grates outside a Harvard building, and Elizabeth Elliot, who has walked to the square to pick up tea and a roll, happen to meet. After a hesitant greeting on both sides, they walk down Brattle Street together toward the Friends Meeting.

Tim is pale. When Elizabeth asks how he feels he answers only with a grunt. She is silent until they reach the top of Longfellow Park, where she turns toward him and says, "I'm very glad you're coming to Meeting. All the problems concerning John's death have been difficult, and I'm sorry if Harriet made you feel unwanted when you were looking for me. She was worried about me, I'm sure. But I hope you know you're welcome with Friends. That's real, Tim, even if we sometimes don't do as well as we should." The two of them turn to cut through the grass of the park and walk on thirty more feet before Tim says, "Thanks for saying that.

You know, nobody at your Meeting has said that kind of thing before."

"I'm sorry," replies Elizabeth, and sorrow is evident in her voice as she adds, "We often don't say the right, and the best, things. I'm going to be Clerk for a long time to come, I think. If anyone here gives you trouble, please come to me."

Tim does not reply, but he smiles to himself. There is a companionable silence between them as they reach the front door of the Meetinghouse.

Elizabeth is warmly, though quietly, greeted by half a dozen Quakers. She sits down near Jane Thompson and not far from Neil Stevenson. She remembers her idea of inviting Neil over to dinner after Meeting but decides this is not a good First-day for entertainment. She puts him quickly out of her mind.

No one speaks or nods to Tim as he enters and he sits alone near the door. After a short time, he gets up and moves to a seat nearer one of the windows that looks out over Longfellow Park. He is trembling slightly and, as oftentimes in Meeting, he looks distressed.

Young Jack Nelson, sitting near the same window as Tim, swings his legs vigorously under the bench until his mother motions him to be still. Elizabeth catches Jack's eye and smiles. He shyly returns the smile and glances up at his mother. Alice has her eyes firmly closed for the moment, trying to concentrate on worship. Seeing this, Jack quickly raises his hand in a wave to Elizabeth, and just as quickly drops the salute. He looks down at the floor and then back up at the Clerk. She smiles a second time but then looks away, not wishing to provoke insubordination in the youngster.

Elizabeth looks for her niece and sees her in a corner of

the room. She looks tired, but her youthful beauty is still clear. Glancing up, Sarah notices neither Elizabeth nor Jack. The undergraduate is fully absorbed in her thoughts. She had arisen painfully early this morning and written a long letter to Steven, explaining she must stop seeing him. She feels it important to follow her own calling in life, and cannot simply adopt a man's professional or religious life for his convenience. Sarah is confident her decision is the right one, but she is sorry to lose Steven. As she sits in Quaker silence, her heart is full of grief and she is near tears.

Bill Hoffman walks across the grass of Longfellow Park, dressed in a gray suit. He enters the Meetinghouse and the Clerk sees him. He looks wan. Bill nods his head toward her and sits next to the fireplace at the end of the room. He crosses his legs, folds his hands, closes his eyes, and sinks into the silence of prayer.

Within a few more minutes the silence of worship begins to deepen and thicken for everyone. It slowly envelops all the people gathered together this Sabbath. Elizabeth sighs quietly with pleasure and begins to feel her tensions ease. The last few weeks have been even more difficult than she has realized and she is glad now to be at home once more in Meeting.

The words of Amos the Prophet come to Elizabeth: "Let justice roll down like the waters." But the notion of justice has never been less clear to Elizabeth than it is now. She hopes that her brothers and sisters in the Meeting, including Tim, will be able to find some strength in the silence that surrounds them. She prays for Adam, now in police custody, and for the Meeting community, as it tries to understand tragedy.

Whatever justice may be, Elizabeth silently asks that

Adam be granted the peace and strength required to survive the ordeal that is now publicly upon him. And she asks for the same for Bill Hoffman, whose uncle tried to throttle a Quaker friend rather than listen to the facts of his nephew's life, and perhaps his own life as well. This past month has shown Elizabeth enormous sadness in the lives of several good Friends. She comforts herself for a moment that she was called to seek the truth and was true to that calling.

Gathering her strength, Elizabeth begins the task of examining her own regrettable behavior over the past several weeks. She remembers all the things she has done which have troubled her conscience. As she listens to the silence surrounding her, some of her melancholy eases and she feels a little hope. Words come into her mind unbidden, words circling around the ideas of justice and a calling. Normally the silence transports Elizabeth above words, but this morning that is not the case. The words swirl within her head and then resolve themselves into a stanza:

> In this sad life we cannot know
> To what we may be called.
> But like the waters, justice flows
> Around and through us all.

Elizabeth Elliot weeps quietly for herself and her friends.

Irene Allen is a geologist with a recent Ph.D. from Harvard University. She lived in Cambridge for six years and is a member of the Religious Society of Friends. She is now at work on her second Elizabeth Elliot mystery.